D0105653

THE LITTLE BOOK

David Hughes

THE LITTLE BOOK

HUTCHINSON
London

This edition first published in 1996 by Hutchinson

Random House (UK) Limited
20 Vauxhall Bridge Road, London SW1V 2SA

Random House Australia (Pty) Limited
20 Alfred Street, Milsons Point, Sydney,
New South Wales 2061, Australia
Random House New Zealand Limited
18 Poland Road, Glenfield, Auckland 10,New Zealand

Random House South Africa (Pty) Limited
PO Box 337, Bergviei, 2012 South Africa

A CIP record for this book is available from
the British Library

Papers used by Random House UK Limited are natural, recyclable
products made from wood grown in sustainable forests. The
manufacturing processes conform to the environmental regulations
of the country of origin.

ISBN 0 09 179194 4

Typeset in by Pure Tech India Ltd., Pondicherry, India.
Printed and bound in Great Britain
by Mackays of Chatham

Lizzo

Chapter One

꧁꧂

These pages are for you.

On a summer Saturday afternoon at home in London I ran upstairs for a pee and blood streamed out. It was the hue of the 1982 Domaine de l'Amarine I had drunk at lunch. Already a relief lurked behind the hot weather. Today would not turn out as planned.

The next hour was normal enough. I took the car to the bottle bank in Kennington Lane and deposited out of plastic bags our last week's detritus. Much of it was empties of the very l'Amarine that now was confused with blood. I monitored any hint of sensation within. I had nothing to report but mild surprise, a fumble between the unexplored and the inexplicable. The afternoon traffic sounded at a remove. I then drove home and pissed wine again.

I lay down for a rest after tea. There was an ache in my lower back, like the almost pleasant imminence of flu. I wondered why I was failing in fits

1

and starts to read some book or other. A pulse, a repetitive blockhead of a pulse, rumbled in my left side far down. A part of my body was singling itself out. I took off all my clothes and slithered into bed. Only when the summer evening backed off, the throb above my buttock starting into a real drum of pain, pang after pang coming deeper and quicker, did I recognize a trick had been played on me.

The trick was to last all night. I had no sleep. I knelt at the rim of the bath vomiting the small hours down the enamel. Washing the sick away with water was the only therapy to hand. I squatted on the lavatory in foetal despair. It appeared that I was being made to behave as someone else intended. Some enemy was extemporizing brutally on my body, making it speak a language of which I had no understanding. At dawn the pain lapsed. I squirmed into a last-minute semblance of sleep that closed over a night that seemed both meant and meaningless.

I awoke that morning to the same shouts in my body which died to a murmur when the duty doctor drugged it with a suppository shoved in by me.

Later I felt the enemy had done with me for the moment. I was lying in emergency at St Thomas's. The simple relief now was to have time back, a return to ordinary speech. My memory was dazed. In

2

good health there had been other moments —
would they recur? — when I thought I was feeling
my way towards a new everything, new language,
new shift in understanding, new modes of playing
my life as though it were a unique instrument.
From now on I accepted that I was being played by
other hands. They wheeled me prone down a cor-
ridor. In the steely lift, eyeing the overhanging
face of the porter, I was content with that fate. I
might soon even learn what was wrong with me
and what I had done wrong.

On my narrow trolley I lay thinking of childhood in Hampshire. I wanted back my particular
share of past. In this tangle with mortality I was
already looking for loose ends to tie up. I thought
of how and when my life had begun to improvise
itself, not be what I wanted. Often in retrospect it
felt the wrong way round, my life. Uncomposed;
variations on a theme never announced. Now
seemed a good time to contemplate the statement
of a theme, if I were not so weak. I had about as
much theme in me as a drowned rat.

At least I was no longer expected to shape
things, only to shape up to them. I was here to take
orders that would be carried out by paid help. The
relief of being in good hands acted as an anaesthetic to anxiety. I first felt the fullness of this relief when an instant bed was found for me. It was

nine floors up in the urological ward, a homecoming. The relief swept over me too during the tests that bore my body day after day down passages into the glare of examination rooms. Irrespective of diagnostic outcome these tests held out a lazy promise of sensuality, me lying helpless in the hands of the staff running the machines, people as casually abrasive as chums, a good enough definition of intimacy until I worked out a better one.

Most protective of all – would this last? – was the crass surge of relief, no, pride, which I felt ten days after the operation to remove a kidney. On the morning I had been told not to take release from hospital for granted the surgeon opened up the threshold of freedom by telling me that the tumour he had cut out, ah yes, the tumour, was indeed, yes, very aggressive, in other words (though not uttering the word) cancer. He was letting me – for better or worse, with every hope of more months, even a year or two, as many as five – go home. Do what you have always wanted to do, he urged, go abroad, explore the world, cram in all the things you have missed.

Again relief washed my brain. For once I had no choice. I had no responsibility to make things happen or prevent them. Events were beyond me. This illness seemed a welcome farewell to the horrors of liberty, of personal decision, of making a mark, of justifying the use of time. I came out on the pavement in high spirits.

One day the future would hit me with the facts. But when exactly?

When?

A morning or two after leaving hospital I was being driven down to the Isle of Wight in amazing heat. I hardly dared trust the novelty of being out and about. I was within short distances of boyhood churches hidden at wooded intervals along the swing of the Meon valley, the unsung organs of which I was still celebrating in the recesses of memory. It was the road of youth.

On this errant road I was feeling my way into the idea that the past was only raw material. It was for turning into whatever I might make of it now. In (as exam papers used to say) the time allowed. Here was a search which must be stepped up. One that had to reach beyond itself.

We drove on.

Between Farringdon and East Tisted, villages once cycled to, the idea crystallized: life and time existed only to have stories spun out of them. Stories of the kind you told in bars to raise laughs, hardly. Stories that put you in a good light at a party, not really. Stories as addictive as drugs that helped you to tolerate life and time, yes, yes. Yet life ought to be more bearable than a story, however much I craved stories.

We accelerated down the valley.

Past Exton and into Corhampton as we sped south, I kept thinking how reality might and must be translated into something beyond its usual tedium. We stopped, everyone clamouring for refreshment. At the pub in Droxford, over the thick sandwiches and beer too potent, I doubted if any pattern in the here-below was to be discovered – none at least that surpassed the efforts of art.

Sweat poured off my eyebrows in the unaccustomed sun. The drink switched into a headache.

But what did stick with me was a need. Or the need for one. The need returned to me on the run into the motorway system writhing around Portsmouth, the need to try out an answer of my own to the question of all this half-remembered muck I had accumulated. I looked out at the chaos of roads and thought of the bagged rubbish of the brain which I dignified with the name of experience. Thus far it added up to zero or did not add up at all.

It had to. It had to be made to.

We turned into the ferry terminal at Old Portsmouth with my mind made up to this challenge.

There was a slight queue. Up the ramp, then on. The slow crossing with the car on a summer afternoon to an island that swelled with interior mystery against the spaces of the sea excited me. It was so pure. It urged on me a sense, after my recent escape from hospital, that I had earned a right to revelation. We drove in the bright air towards Seaview. I looked forward to the moments to come that would rise above the plod of daily recuperation, the measured pleasures, the outings with a stick. I looked forward to my good intentions.

We were that August in a house perfect for sensuous invalidity. I faced a good sweep of the Solent through long windows, a heap of pillows at my back. We were within a philosophic stroll of a pub where the bitter was well kept and you could lunch in the sun. A short drive away, at a jetty in a tidal harbour, was moored a barge that sold good fish. The village store was packed with wines from half the world. Now and then I wondered if and when it would strike me that all this fun and fare, the peace that stretched to infinity beyond the largesse of the windows, was not destined to last much longer. But for a day or two it did, as the sky toyed endlessly with light, and I marked time beside the seaside, juggling with the past.

I lay in bed that first morning and I thought of you downstairs. I thought of times we had enjoyed together, the recesses of you I missed, the parts of me I never gave you. As I lay weakly looking at the sea, I saw us in each other's arms. There were always things I would have much liked you to know, without having to say them. Here on the Island, dearest, I remembered that I set out when we met years ago with the idea of one day writing the unwritable bible for you. It was to take the form of a little book. It was to be the little book that told you everything in such a way as to make you feel good, better than good, your best. I wanted you to have it among your things, so that if we weren't together for the rest of your life you would always know what I meant with the whole of mine. Our gospel.

So it was to be only for you. It was the big exploratory act which any man wanted to share with his love when he crossed an ocean or street in search of a bit of eldorado. It was the letter that said it all and hid everything, the late-night call across a variety of continents when everyone else was tongue-tied in sleep. It was the complicated child or children we were to share the sharp onus of having, and you and me snatching every chance to meet — those oysters at lunch in Marseilles, timing it well at Chicago airport, luxuriating in Portuguese afternoons — our hearts beating to a quickstep, bodies rising to each other's scent. It was naked bedrooms. It was the mood of music at its most sugary and sharp, the propriety of love at its most improper, the key to the uncrackable mystery of every damn thing we clapped eyes on, the truth as never hitherto known. And most of all it was me in my glory, you in yours, our absurd joint glory. A testament.

But such a book was still unwritable. So, alone in bed, to fetch my mind back from the outer space of illness, I thought I would fall back on telling you and myself, keeping it quiet, the story of what happened when someone else bloody well sat down and had the nerve to write the unwritable.

This little book of someone else's came out of nowhere. It was so simple that at first glance it seemed meant for children, ours or anyone's. It was also quite short, in fact no longer than the pages you now have in your hands. And it was called, of course, *The Little Book*. This work never buttonholed: no hint of sermon or declaration of the obvious, no flights of the lyrical pretending to be as deep as music, no epigrams disguised as wisdom, no nonsense. It had a still centre.

Indeed, if read aloud in the slack of night by a thoughtful adult, I guessed, the book would tempt him, or her, if not both, to take a wholly different view of practically everything, not least of their many selves. And willingly to grit their teeth for change, the change that only the book could wreak. If they wanted it enough.

A book to end books.

All day my mind feinted with it, this bold fantasy: the little book that said it all. Again the idea rushed over me as we drove quietly along the Military Road on the south of the Island past Brook. Look up into the hills at that big house, I thought. There once lived a hero of mine, a fat, gruff, bald hero who typed at a furious pace in a study overlooking the cliffs that cut their blind chalk into the sea at sunset. Priestley at Brook Hill: the only time I ever gave consideration at length to another human being, with enough cheek and verve to write about his gift for turning our ordinary world into an extraordinary one of his own. I used to enter into all his work with spirit, while not apparently like him at all. Inside me there must have been, might still be, a haunting self that wanted to resemble him as much as possible. All my big unrealized projects sprang from my response to the breadth and depth of the horizons in Priestley's view from his study across Tennyson Down and far out to sea. I had known this Island in my youth when I was unformed, protean, a lad of many parts, none of which had forced a way to the front.

Now I was back here to consider what dying was likely to mean to me.

Feeling convalescent, its back against the pillows, its eyes on the ups and downs of the sea, waiting for one slight meal or digesting another, *The Little Book* kept swimming in and out of these early days of recovery.

It was clear that the book was to come out gently during a torrid summer. We potential readers were struck down by heat. Tempers frayed. Flies gathered on the uneasy afternoons. The deep cool of the book, it seemed, could only condense at night – by which time I was often asleep and failing to remember dreams.

The book slipped out of my hand. And hit the floor.

I kept missing the point.

The anonymous author began by saying that his name was not on the spine because I, the reader, now had to make my own book. It was too late for any professional writer to do it for me. He could offer me a bit of guidance, some know-how. But the book was really in my own mind, and it was my heart that knew what it wanted to say. I was free at last – of the tyranny of words or of any other rule.

This sounded like a simple challenge for anyone, especially as the volume was slim, taking a tabloid reader only about an hour to get through. It was the length of a television docudrama, a stint of digging in a retired Hampshire garden, an after-dinner snooze near the Oval on a Sunday, a buffet snack on an Inter-City to Carlisle, a political rally in a cold hall to the west of Brecon, a round or two of large whiskies in good company, a cross-country walk between Seaview and Bembridge, a psychiatric session off Knightsbridge at seventy pounds a time, a sail on Derwentwater or a drive into Welsh hills, a domestic quarrel all over the place, or making slow love anywhere in the world.

Reading the book was, in fact, the right length for anything anywhere. Nothing need ever be longer again, either longer than the fuck or larger than the whiskies or healthier than the sail or more argumentative than the rally or tastier than the snack or dreamier than the snooze or more satis-factorily egocentric than the hour on the couch.

This book, in other words, was to fit the human predicament like a birthday suit. I really longed to know who wrote it, if only because I had this feel-ing I had written it myself.

I want to hold you in my arms in the panic of the night, the book said. In the gloom of day I want to draw you into the sun. The book bit. And pleased. And hurt. A sentence promised to break your heart unless you preferred it to make you laugh. A paragraph kicked you backwards as a preliminary to giving you full support.

The first pages claimed that all the author could do was allow me the ghost of a chance to be myself. To make up my own stories as though telling them to a child. The campfires of the old narrative way were dowsed for ever; the gaudy courts of my mind needed a jester no more. Meanwhile this author could teach me some tricks of the trade, if I were ready to learn.

I thought at first I might be alone in responding to this novelty of approach, but apparently not. I gathered that the book was about to penetrate the meagre remnants of our culture, enter muddled attics in town and basements exuding a provincial damp, skulk half-read within country mansions crumbling nobly into penury, hover over the close-carpeted areas of defunct metropolitan privilege, filter too into many a bedroom where mattresses creaked under a voluptuous want of hope. All these locations, I understood, were embraced in a text of delectable ordinariness, which wished only to be as helpful as it could to one and all in this time of special stress.

The text contained, as perhaps no book ever had, the span and trajectory of life, the wilderness of it, its lack of grammar, its ever-present absence, its refusal to be pinned down or fenced in, as well as the painful, unprogrammed amiability of life, not to mention life's way of creeping out of the silent gaps between the words as abruptly as a genius with blood on his hands, not excluding life's criminal aptitude for giving you the wrong answer with a smile of complacency, plus several other things that laid the mystery wide open only to close it up more firmly than ever; and doing all that, which the book suggested wasn't nearly enough, with a consuming passion.

Sometimes the book struck a sentence as long as the above and seemed to get nowhere. Mostly because readers like myself assumed out of habit that it had nowhere to go.

But I was wrong, my love.

Chapter Two

❧

On the Island, time and again, when flustered, seeking calm, in the lavatory, eyes half open, scar aching, I found obsessively returning this idea of *The Little Book*.

It had a voice of its own, not mine.

Please read with care, it said. Yes, the author had adopted a technique to exact from me an effort no less creative than his. To stop me being lazy. To get my imagination out of the rut.

First, I had to consider this very page a blank, a blank on which my private patterns were forming. By closing my eyes over it, I could see myself at a distance, as one character or another in a story that belonged only to me.

Keep my eyes closed, the book said. Picture someone almost forgotten whom I once met – glimpsed – briefly knew – sat beside in school – went once to bed with in the dark – saw showing off across a crowded room: someone anyway from the saharas of my past. Someone a bit like me.

Someone now plump and sixtyish, early

promise long since gone but braving it out. Thin-nish plumes of grey windblown hair. A downbeat gait, as if no longer on the make or increasingly on the gin. A dark raddled glance projecting an authority not to be denied by waiters, girls, taxi-drivers, snobs, etc. Voice deeply coloured like the best honey. A high brow off which he never stops wiping the sweat of his illusions. A fellow who is alive because still debating how to live.

I've certainly seen him, if only in half-dreams, in myself when my eyes are closed, even in the mirror shaving: a human being who might have done any-thing at a pinch.

The men or women he might have been!

Not just the obvious jobs for one of my disposi-tion, lettered, print-mad, editor of *This* or pub-lisher of the more influential *That*, commanding sober opinion in a post-prandial flow of leaders, but any outcome from packer to premier, any of the disguises available to us all, donning robes to pre-tend to teach, descending from the intoxications of high table to mould the soggy mind of youth, as-suming garb in church to foist a lack of belief in a divinity on the ungodly multitude, putting on ser-vice uniform to control a force trained to greet for-eigners with a hail of bullets, or in the lawcourts, the classrooms, the executive suites, togged up in suits and ties that varied only according to income or pretension, playing a docile part in any of the many professions that needed their assumptions jogged, logic nudged, standards elbowed, by some as yet undiscovered shift.

But all this muddled man did was to write a book – *The Little Book*, to be precise. He had uncannily given away his identity in the first few pages by asking me to imagine him. So of course I leapt to the conclusion that he was meant to be me. Probably untrue. But at least he convinced me that he was down there in the unspeakable depths of myself and had been waiting a very long time to come up.

It was just as much a shock, my love, as meeting you for the first time that day in Wales. Discovering how scattered we were, into how many different compartments we had fractionalized our lives, knowing that now we at least had the chance to be as one, at one.

There seemed no need to choose a name for this author. Here he was in the ample flesh, filling the screen of the inner eye, a friend of mine, doing the nice things I might have done or would be doing now if not unwell: alone in a pungent Marseilles eating fish off the grill and wanting a woman more than anything except more cold wine; softly longing for a long walk in soft English country; snoozing rank afternoons away in the decline of a palazzo

17

near Tivoli; in Barcelona at night wanting the icy tingle of mineral water down his throat more than anything, except the woman.

He was all over the place, this version of myself. As hard to locate as the woman, as vulgarly loud as one of the cities, as romantically gentle as the downland walk, as full of disordered dreams as the snooze, as intoxicating in company as the wine, and as self-indulgent as the lunch. He was a Mediterranean seaport, a castle close to Rome, English acres, an island off the South Coast. He was all these places at once – a continent of a man, as muddled as Europe, who was apparently on the point of vanishing, as if not wanting to face the music, despite the fact that he had himself called the tune.

That first Sunday we attended matins at a church on an eminence inland. Between the roll of chalk hills the sea in the distance was caught by flecks of light. A thanksgiving? Yes, yes, if only for being still here to give thanks.

A crotchety organ played me back to boyhood. The exhausted phrases of the Venite bored into my memory. I sat numbed, tired out, cast down in loss, caught up again in time. I gave no thought to *The Little Book* as the psalms droned away and summer hummed outside. From where I sat in a muddle names chiselled out of death lay flat on the floor or cut into tablets on the walls, relating in marriage and oblivion families that once owned half the island. We had a wobbly rendering of the Te Deum to a chant I failed to recognize.

The vicar mounted the pulpit. His sermon arose from a fatigued text, and fell away, and rose again from the dead, and nodded off, declining slowly into a murmur that mingled with the comfortable suggestions of eternity over the fields and far away, and then, eyes closing, we all stood up for the last hymn. I gazed round, awaited the blessing, longing to get outside, breathe, get home, lie down, lie low.

To evade the vicar's handshake at the porch we looked round his church. Against the north wall, near a doorway blocked in the Middle Ages to prevent entry by the devil, was propped a pair of hassocks embroidered with poppies below a small lectern bearing a large leatherbound book. The book devoted a printed page each to all the sons of the parish who had died in both world wars. The foreword modestly proposed that the old refrain of 'we will remember them' made sense only if you knew how they had spent their lives before laying them down. Long infancies, a few terms in school, a girl quickly done under a hedge, a short sharp job as smithy or labourer. Then war.

The church behind me was utterly still. Never before had I seen such a careful memorial to men who had cared enough to risk all they had. Opposite the summary biographies, two decades of living compressed into a couple of hundred words, stood odd stanzas of poems, Brooke softening the blow, Sassoon berating the generals, Owen tightening a garotte on sentiment. From a few lanes round this church they went out to Norway, Gallipoli, Newfoundland, Bombay, the Somme, Gaza, to help lay waste the wider world in the name of a value nobody had quite worked out. To read the book was as painful as any of my efforts to gather those wars into myself: the boys had lived within a hundred yards of here, as close as an enemy trench. In the noon lull I stood quietly in the church being sniped at by history.

Those wars still stuck with me, a cancer in the craw. All the lives spilt from this island seemed to cohere into one person – an unknown soldier, complimented for bravery, congratulated on his suffering, commended for anonymity. This was the man who went out under the same colours as, and with similar emotions to, and with hardly less implacable a purpose than, millions like him: individuals, but only in the making. In peace his eye had wavered over a choice of career. He was trying his hand at being a gardener, a baker, a blacksmith, and now he was trained for a spell into stoker, marine, tommy. Ahead of him, in theory, had lain every possibility. He could have become anyone. And all his stories were told in that volume only because those futures of his were cut off. He lost all the chances, except of being remembered. The man who could have been anything, and gone anywhere, ended up being recalled, from a book, this summer Sunday on the Island, by me.

Out in the churchyard the stones once stood upright. The parish had flattened centuries of burial to make a lawn. A few survivors with crumbled lettering were embedded in ranks along the wall of the manor house, the motorized cutting of grass the only sound this summer noon. From one corner led a narrowing vista of gravestones left standing, an area blackly overhung by the claws of flyblown evergreens. These trees seemed stark with warning, gibbets almost. I ventured into the dense grass that veiled most of the graves. More deeply lost even than the cock-eyed crosses or stove-in tombs was an open book in marble blotched by lichen, the inscription decayed, the small leaden letters wrenched out by time, leaving behind only a smudged hollow. It lay on the ground open at the middle saying nothing under grasses past their prime. Even spreading your details across an apparently permanent page was no guarantee.

Via Adgestone and Brading I was driven from the high solitude of the downs home to sea level, still thinking of that one man dying in war who stood in for so many persons denied their chance. I saw him as myself, of course. The kick of identifying gave point to my life. Here I was off to the wars. Here was the horse and cart taking us all into town to volunteer. We believed to the fingertips in the cause. Naturally we all had different names, though as likely as not we were all at removes of the same family, the humble among us to be rubbed out in the churchyard just as surely as those resplendently lettered on the transept floor. But now we were launched back into life. At the last minute we were being asked to save our country, then, snatched back from the abyss, to come home as heroes and make that country fit for us to live in.

I thought back over my own family's many names. Hughes was of recent date; we had been Parry well into the nineteenth century. Parry, ap Harri, son of Harry. My mother was a Cochrane, hers a Dickinson; further back skulked a Darley. Gran was called Mary Ann Latimer Fielden until she married Owen William Hughes. All these names I could juggle with, just as did the

memorials in that village where everyone was related to everyone else. All our names belonged to
me for the asking. I was part of all of them; rather
were they parts of me I had hardly bothered, was
too indolent, to spot or recognize.

But I could take advantage of them. Recall these
ancestors if only by name. Use them to personify
those other people I might so easily have been: the
persons who in ironic guises were now to step into
the ambience of *The Little Book*.

And read it. Or get the action going. Or ignore it,
burn it, stage a demo about it, pepper the papers
with 'Disgusted' of wherever, report it to the
police or make it the subject of a Private Member's
Bill, set it to students, discourage postgraduates in
Canada from writing theses about it, roger a PhD
on packets of remaindered copies of it, or give it
the DSO for outstanding bravery, raise it to the
peerage or nominate it for a safe seat in the Com-
mons. The Latimer in me, coastal Yorkshire stock,
would put up with none of *The Little Book*'s nonsense. The Fielden, from Wensleydale, would
marvel at its cheek. The Dickinson part of me,
from the nicer suburbs of Eastbourne, would look
down the nose at the rude words that disguised the
nastier thoughts. I could rely on the Cochranes for
rough justice, my grandpa a dredger captain, his
brother a sherry addict. The Parrys were lost in

time's least privileged womb quarrying slate in North Wales, but worth dragging back to the present for their honesty and premature death. And there were probably other relatives to plunder.

As we wriggled our way back down the lanes into the comforts of Seaview after worshipping at that upland church, I wondered why it had taken me so long to realize how many of my relations were up in arms inside me, longing to express the force of their views, biding their moment until I was too weak to protest, impelling my imagination to admit them to counsels hitherto kept secret, barging in as of right. For the moment I was too exhausted by motion and by time to have an answer before the rigmarole of siesta, tea, drinks, supper, nightcap, bed, let alone before lunch.

Here on the Island I liked the idea of inventing myself all over again under as many aliases as I fancied. It gave me some way to go. I longed for another outing. You suggested it next day with some doubt. It involved walking uphill. From the car park it was a slow, uneven walk on a lane rising to the grand house at Appuldurcombe, and I took it in spasms, resting on my stick in the wayside verdure as others passed, a clownish Lazarus giving a demonstration of the difficulty of motion. But I

had insisted on the trip, once mooted. I fancied
horizons other than the sea.

This mansion inland was gravely handsome,
dating from an era of elegance, but only a shell, at
some time gutted by fire. Attempts had been made
to reconstruct one or two rooms within, to reflect
the gracious living. But some floors were still of
grass and much of the domestic space was hollow:
lawned saloons that echoed to the bare rafters with
the voices of unseen youngsters that came from an
age I had outlived. A tall figure in the prime of
middle age, darkly spry in a light suit, passed out
of sight across a doorway. For a moment I almost
thought I half recognized him: a younger self perhaps, brisk of step, clearly in better shape. Or
someone from a shop or bar in Seaview. But all
these visitors looked as though they were bypas-
sing me. They were in another world, edging me
out of mine.

My family wanted more of the interior so, exhausted, I sat out in the gardens on an infirm
bench. Elegant too were these layouts of bedded
annuals in the crook of gravel curves, but only just
holding on: a faded aquatint of their heyday. Flies
heavily active stirred over the stagnant pond that
was meant as a fountain, insects brooding and
breeding on flat leaves of water lilies gone limp.
I stared up at the blue. Again in my somnolence I

wondered if my life made a story; or if I could shake a story out of the raw material of that life; or if this life were doomed to mean nothing, whatever I did. I gazed with unease back at the house. A damsel-fly hovered. Goodness, I felt sleepy, in this ancient sun and desuetude. The very heat hummed messages I had no way of fathoming.

As if memories were mirages.

Only vaguely knowing who or where I was, I seemed to be thinking that rumours of *The Little Book* had begun circulating in London well before publication that summer.

One or two hints drifted into the Sunday newspaper whose literary editor was a busy careerist of roughly my age called – what? Hugh Dickinson, brisk, in good shape, besuited. Having for short periods held down such jobs on papers, I could imagine for myself, with the ease of familiarity, this handsome chap enjoying his middle age. Indeed I had observed hints of him everywhere in my life. Sketches of him in dark suits belonged to my club, where his kind of well-turned professional offered me tempting terms for life insurance, arranged my divorce, submitted plans for an addition to my house, sneaked into bed with my mistress, told me stories at the bar: a friend to everyone.

And at once I realized what *The Little Book*'s

author meant. Dickinson was no different from me, of course. Or part of me: a middling middle-class muddle, as cunning as the lawyer and stressed as the architect; any Englishman doing his job with interest, but bored, living his life with vigour, but distressed, giving his family what they seemed to need, but anxious; prowling in search of something else, something at the luminous back of a dim beyond, but doubtful.

However, if his present life said nothing to this Hugh Dickinson, how could a little anonymous book be expected to say more?

'Who is this nobody?' he said moodily to the office at large.

He was told that the author's identity was perhaps known to only one person, a girl, a reportedly hot number who ran fact and fiction in the house that was soon to publish *The Little Book*.

Dickinson arranged to lunch with this dubious paragon, who turned out to have polished eyes as hard as turquoises. They seemed stonily fixed on him as though to hide faults or secrets. Obviously, like the restaurant which he used for convenience, she had gone down a lot. Her sexual muscle was doubtless as limp as the asparagus.

But there was something about her which Dickinson caught himself not wanting to see and she was contained by this odd indefinable, seemingly fulfilled by it: a purr of inner entertainment which he had no wish to share; in fact he felt like smashing it to pieces. For it looked smug, it calmed her face too much. And of course it had to do with the privacies of *The Little Book*.

'You'll see,' she said.

'Tell me more.'

'I'm not being coy,' she replied coyly. 'But I honestly can't explain. Just wait until you read it.'

Her eyes continued to gaze at him with a feral steadiness that was also moral. And unnerving. He spilt a driblet of wine while pouring more of the second bottle. She had introduced into his stomach a sense of physical dissolution, which made him feel flatly exploited, as after self-abuse. And still without a blink she stared at him out of some more luminous world which aroused in him both guilt and desire, each lewdly feeding on the other in a combination that made his knees spongy.

'Unseen powers?' His voice wobbled.

'Could be.'

But she would divulge no clue to the book's purpose or provenance, let alone the author's name. 'You'll see,' she said again divinely, teeth closing over a final strawberry.

Dickinson wanted to pain her for being so knowingly superior. Yet they cabbed at speed back to her flat, got entangled in boozy undressing, and were in the thick of making love with the detached application of dogs when into the room came a fat man.

They subsided on the sheet. Dickinson thought, Christ, husbands, the old story. He experienced spasms of withdrawal and much incipient hostility.

The fat man's face inside the door looked amicably anonymous in the gloom until with a delayed yelp she said, 'Go away,' whereupon the fellow laughed without rancour and answered, 'Well, old thing, we're all made of the same stuff, I take it, when all's said and done, share and share alike, good luck to the sod', knocked a pot of violets off a chest, swayed briefly to resume his bearings, exited crabwise with a muffled apology, waved a plump hand and vanished.

Who was this character? Since he evidently had her key, might he not also be author of the book that meant so much to her? So he was real after all. At this nudge of suspicion the desire all muddled up on the bed lost heart. Issues more serious obtruded. Oh fuck, thought Dickinson limply.

I awoke when almost asleep. I had been gazing through heavy lids at the frontage of Appuldurcombe. Flies settled for a second, whizzed off. I had no idea what came next in the story. I was too dazed by fatigue. I only wished that just once I had lived in such a house as this, in my prime and its, a place that savoured its age. To occupy the shell of a great house, to rebuild, to furnish rooms within its open spaces, to expand into its possibilities, to stamp myself upon the magnificence of its breeding, to pay for it all, to paint its sweeps of wall and mask its deficiencies, to make it the repository of my secrets, to amplify the ghosts that walked its passages, to embed it in the degree of cultivation that served the aesthetic needs of such a pile, to pass it on to the children as their hiding-place, to serve sumptuous meals within the ample spaces for dining, to offer the hospitality of its creaking floorboards to friends illicitly in love, to uphold its traditions with a plethora of servants, I would have had to have turned out to be, or turn myself into, a different man.

Why hadn't I?

Why didn't I?

By now, lying in bed at Seaview, creating characters out of myself and entering their lives, I was following *The Little Book*'s precepts with relative ease. I recognized the source of that publisher's moll with the feral smile. She had been coquetting in my backstage thoughts for years: the fantasy girl I never quite met, let alone had.

I still hadn't had her, dammit. She lounged un-assaulted on the tenebrous couches of the mind, a girl whose prepubescent face slyly freshened the rear benches in class, whom I glimpsed in adoles-cence on a pavement from a bus, to whom I was given no introduction at a party, who always quitted my future at just the moment I entered it.

I dressed her up. And undressed her. Laid her over my knees and kissed her. Spanked her. Wor-shipped her with fury. Bought seamy magazines for a haphazard glimpse of those eyes rolling back into her head at my touch. The quite impossible she. As much a part of me as any of my so-called selves.

So I named her Davina Darley and decided to make her the mouthpiece not only of my own in-carcerated desires, but of the precise effect of *The Little Book* on the murmurously chaotic intui-tions of all those women in Britain who were to read it that summer.

Davina . . .

'I suppose I have to read this damn book,' Dickin-son said ruefully, putting on his trousers.

'No,' she said with unexpected verve. 'No. You don't read a book like this. It's not a book. It's a ravening wolf. It chases you through the dark forests of yourself. You try to run away from it –

but you're not fit enough. It tracks you down. You hope to goodness it's stopped howling at you, but then suddenly it springs. And you're lost.'

'Or found,' he said for effect.

She nodded vigorously. Dickinson bent over the bed to embrace her almost naked body, if only to convey the elation her words stirred in him, but she eluded his grasp. 'Now what does it say about sex being irresponsible and childish?' she said in forbidding tones. 'No, that's just the sort of rational thing the book is clever enough not to say. That's why I have the impression it says it.'

'Between the lines?'

'Don't be so obvious. It has outdated that concept at a stroke.'

'How does it say it then?'

She frowned, as at a dunce. 'It says everything original in a way that's such a whacking platitude that nobody notices it,' she said. 'They just sense it. They feel the originality. It goes straight to the guts, the words actually get down there and fight, they give you that kick in the belly and you rush to your doctor for pills in a tizz – except that it's only well-being. It's just you, you coming alive for the first time, and you can't stand the shock, can you?'

Dickinson blinked. The fantasy girl was rebelling. It struck him that she must be trying to find substitute language, and failing, for something inexpressible which the book simply expressed. The words were probably as natural and fleeting as a species of weather, just gusts, currents on a page that blew into you, small shadowy signs that brought out your sun.

And then, as if reading his thoughts, she said, 'The book says everything you want it to, then a bit more which is a nice bonus, then a lot more than you can bear, and finally it gives you our old world in a new guise of beauty and bounty, and then that too turns out not to be ultimate either, because, in spite of being short, the book keeps going on and on by apparently using fewer and fewer words, until you find to your horror — and this is the happiest moment of all — that it's using no words whatever, hasn't used any, won't use any, and the whole miracle has been taking place in the purity of your own imagination, which has needed just that release all your life.'

'And you still won't tell me who wrote it?'

'You did. I did. Any old reader did. I can't tell you more. Oh, what does it matter?'

He kissed her, on the cheek, formally. Despite being a bit vexed by her runic evasions, Dickinson had never felt more originally in love with anyone, or indeed with himself, which seemed to count more: lots of himself in varying versions, a tangle of selves about to untie and live on their own at last. He was conscious of an explorer's tense delight in having a long way to go before an elysium miraged out of the ice or desert. All this appeared to lie silent within the unconfined future of the book.

'I'll bike you a copy this afternoon,' she said, and for the first time, as she openly swung legs off the bed, he saw the innocently impersonal dark folds of her parts. It was as touching as childhood. He wanted abruptly to bury his head in the intricacies of it all.

On the Island, waking up sharply just after dawn, I saw that this was the first magnificent weekend of a summer that was to parch the landscape and change the entire face of the country. As usual on Saturdays, his pages on the paper put to bed, Hugh Dickinson caught the train down to his mansion among the trees of the south. *The Little Book* was in the briefcase on the rack, a time-bomb or a damp squib.

He arrived home. He loved that house. There was a slant of late coppery sunlight on the boles of chestnuts, which seemed to forecast evanescently a repetitive eternity of children, summers, wives, anxieties, alcohol. The front door was open as if for ever on the dying light. The family supped early on stew. The children manufactured lots of private mischief, then in public protest refused to go to bed. Then went to bed.

Dickinson said, 'I love you.'

'I love you,' said his wife.

Which mostly meant that they had both been drinking wine, one they relished from foreign holidays and could now obtain locally – though it did not taste the same, though they did not say so. Years of complicity lay as safe as an abyss between them.

Dickinson opened a door on to his lawns and stared at the lemony aftermath of sunset defining the hills. Like a ghost, tremulously, an owl started to woo the forthcoming night. He shuddered, feeling for a second on the brink of the other side of the normal, wherever that was. He simultaneously felt the urgency of some task to perform – the book, yes, reading the book – which in some way unrevealed but intimate had to do with this customary world dropping away from the sunset into dark and silence.

The kitchen clattered faintly behind him, things were draining. An evening home was in danger of passing away into the rot of routine, tomorrow's unwanted plans, yawns, flaccid hints of a lust departed; then deep sleep, troubled by a tangle of dreams.

But, no, he walked in from the darkness and

plucked out of his briefcase the copy of *The Little Book* and pushed the first page under the lamp.

What incalculable reality was stirring in Dickinson as the book set his imagination to work? By God, he was being asked to invent out of his own mess another person altogether.

For a handful of those first sentences Dickinson was half aware of himself living uneasily in the ease of the country after a soft week in the hardness of town. Inner muscles were relaxing under the massage, not only of good words exactly positioned, but of the familiarity of his setting dulled into place by drink. He was at home, at night, at rest. But he was also somewhere else.

As for me so for him, the experience did not resemble reading at all. The pages echoed back to him, as if entering recesses of his private thought which he had never suspected, all the trifles of everyday which he believed he had enjoyed during that week, but had missed by a mile: the office never quite dull but bloody near it; the grace of falling asleep under the thud of rain; the steady tread of his feet going places for good reasons, over carpets, on pavements gilded by lamplit drizzle, up flights of stairs; greeting someone known for years, making with a cool drink in the hand all the fond allowances, and that witty spark of anticipation when evenings dawned; buds, decisions, odours of earth, eyes in the street; the primal flush of blossom shortlived against a wall glimpsed out of a taxi, a wash of blue above narrowing perspectives, a purchase in a shop, soap, book, blade, pen, a commonplace; a girl decisively drinking him in with blue eyes in bed, the buds of her nipples, peace, peace; and a short while later the very ordinariness of the office, never dull but almost. Life, in fact. Instants of blind pleasure. To be savoured into a pattern. To be valued into a balance. To be lived.

From these pages Dickinson knew that he had recently had the effrontery to live a week's life as though it were of no possible consequence.

Or indeed not happening at all.

Chapter Three

❧

Darling, at this point in my reading of *The Little Book*, just when my imagination begins to tingle, I sit back for a moment cushioned on the Isle of Wight, finding it hard to encompass how much of our own lives together the book, without argument, persuades me we have lost. And only time will tell how much has drained uselessly out of us over the years when we were pursuing aims and ambitions that in no way reflected the people we were or wanted to be. I find this to be stunning news. Nobody ever clarified it before.

Usually my perception of reading was that words just ate neatly into the surface of the brain. But these words, with a subversive gluttony, had somehow set their teeth to work on the unconscious. They gorged on my soul.

I did not know what to think – or whether, as the book seemed to prefer, not to think anything.

I closed my eyes, as advised, with a view to having them opened, as promised.

Confronting me, sitting there at home in the small
hours of a country house, the said Hugh Dickinson felt to his consternation that he was in touch
with others. They were all inside him. It was hard
to tell what they were trying to communicate; they
felt like districts of himself that were crying out to
be realized. For those words on the lighted page
had been luminously transmuted, not into
thought in the well-mannered fashion of good
prose, but straight into emotion. Or was it emotion? If not, what moved and humoured him so
much?

He could frame no answers; indeed believed without question that he wasn't meant to. It just seemed
vital to feel his way beyond feeling into some other
areas as yet uncharted. He recognized aghast that he
had changed overnight, in depths of which he had
been criminally unaware, but also in several obvious
ways that implied a degree of ascetic refinement
hardly believable in a man so loosely self-indulgent
for so long: smoking, eating, drinking, sleeping,
fucking, all too much – he had liked it all far too
much.

Yet here was the book making him want to
avoid sleep, despite a potent longing to dream; it
roundly put him off all thoughts of a square meal,
turned him against alcohol's power to smother his
brains in anaesthetic, turned the inhalation of a

cigarette into choking on sewage: thus the idea of kissing someone, making her body spring to the touch, now smacked repulsively of sleep, smoke, meat, shit, booze. All the old compulsive pleasures convulsed in sickness within him – he had over-used them. Or never used them honestly.

Also the book seemed to query the very concept of wives and children by casting doubt on the nature of his love for them. And it forced him to question beauty (the way a landscape or a body suggested it), time (the way a clock ticked it), and people (the way they insisted on being). Finally it bit pounds of flesh out of his assumptions all round.

But despite being starved, drained of desires, done out of drinks, short on sleep, doubtful of love, denied a future as emptily nice as the past, or because of these things, Hugh Dickinson knew that the book had made him feel more commandingly alive than ever before. It was speeding the blood in his arteries, scouring the trash out of his brain, throwing light on pitchblack gulfs of him that were beyond the reach of time. It had switched off his ego; and thus shown him a glimpse of something hitherto undisclosed (what was it?) to the inner eye; and was pioneering a vision (what was it?), that would one day come clean. For the moment it was enough to believe from the bizarre prose of *The Little Book* that such a vision (where was it?) existed.

For somewhere here was supernature staring into his eyes as transparently as a watermark on a page.

This evening on the Island the ultra smart and young drifted past our jetty on their way to dinner parties before the Dinghy Dance. We were at the social climax of the Regatta. Evening wear in daylight – girls on the beach path in black stockings textured by the setting sun, jewellery as dazzling as the waves – had a disturbing glamour. Studs glittered under black ties. Without envying their youth I was jealous of their interminable lives. And, sharing their sense of occasion, I began to summon up the tremendous party the publishers were giving to launch *The Little Book*, digging the celebration of a lifetime out of the scraps jostling in my memory.

Shut your eyes and enjoy yourself, the book said, and all the high sunsets and dusks of festivity I had accumulated over the years flooded into place, an inner cornucopia of village hops, receptions, garden parties, outings to the seaside, balls: my earlier life of noisy pleasure upped by a few decibels and drinks and doubts. For it was evident that this party was to be peopled by my past.

As ordered I closed my eyes. I saw the tipsy old images of excess shaking down into a pattern. I saw an eggshell fragility in the beauty of the evening, as in a city on the brink of war. All occasions were unique. The picture cleared as excitingly as a precedent.

In an enclave of inner London, the party overspilling the publisher's offices on to shadowed pavements, many guests I seemed half to know were assembling in twilit groups. As yet I could hardly see their faces. Flares burning on standards threw a race of huge reflections across the arcades of the market. Sawn-off barrels were set at intervals, packed high with ice, stuffed with champagne. Hands I had once held gripped the necks of bottles. Tongues I had tongued wagged in cheeks. Eyes made war.

A party to end parties.

I stared at the figures taking shape in front of me in the uncertain light. Apart from Hugh Dickinson, who loomed knowingly amid this fuzzy elite, none of them had read *The Little Book*, but they were here to see it in like a New Year, to bellow it in, crowd it out, think it through, talk it down, feel it up and drink it to death. Here suddenly was D.J. House, an Oxford professor of history, lofty, storkish, gesticulating in the background, honouring the book by grandly abstaining from absence. Over there, securing for the book the imprimatur of the leisured classes, stood the thin shape of Sir Davis Fielden, so remote as to be almost elsewhere, accompanied at a remove by his even more otherworldly wife. Latimer Johns MP, a junior minister, kept to the distinguished rear of the party so that I could hardly make out his features, the dark jowl, balding head, long nose of the cartoons: a caricature who represented me in parliament. The saturnine Owen Parry, warehouse foreman to the book's publisher, was forgettably handing round drinks on the fringes. Girls who had waltzed through my life at some point gazed unseeingly. Men I had once esteemed stared past me into a future that darkened minute by minute.

And down the street alongside the party, looking in, sidled one Dave Higgs, uninvited, disabled by drink, unhinged by his hate of the pleasure of others, pinching a copy as he moved on.

To think that this cavalcade of arrogance stood in for my past! I had no means of evading it. Here they all were, nodding at me curtly, waving without affection, passing me on a waft of perfume, looking at me askance out of contexts long soured, reconstituting passions I thought I had forgotten, reviving ambitions I assumed I had grown out of: selfishly pursuing their ends, as if trying to elude me. I had tried both to like them and to be like them, and on both counts failed. They had been the gawky agents of my growing up. Surely I had matured away from their temporary charms by now and become my chosen self.

But I hadn't. The book's residue in my veins told me that I had clumsily mislaid these people along the way. At various points, years ago, they had dropped away from me, and I had missed them, and it hurt, and I had refused or been unable to see that by leaving them behind, by suppressing their very different modes and tempers within me, I was becoming progressively less than myself: even more of a child than ever because I had let them fade out. And in the act of blocking them off, or not pursuing through them what I might have become, or not deliberately killing them to the last vestige, I had lost my direction.

Yet of course they owed me nothing. They were not people. I had never taken the trouble to create them properly, to give them birth, send them about their business, forget them. They remained stuck in my innards, a neurotic amalgam of expense accounts, wasted afternoons, errors of judgement, crude acts of narcissism, failures of contact, betrayals and bad jokes. No wonder they scarcely seemed to recognize me as I tried to recall who they were.

Nonetheless they had composed my life – such as it was, the book gently reminded me.

The Dinghy Dance also went on late into the night. From our jetty it echoed out to sea in a muted roar, music bumping beneath the laughter. I wandered down the street for a closer look. Youngsters fell jokily out of the doorway of the Yacht Club, picked up their rhythm, danced off towards the shore. Into the club, his mien urgent, hair disordered by his speed of progress, dashed the black-tied figure of a man I had often seen loping the streets on enterprises unknown. He looked academic. His build suggested eager research, a longing to beat a rival at his own infinitesimal game. It lodged in my mind with a click of recognition that this was the unstable but respected Professor House, whose presence at the launch of *The Little Book* had seemed improbably vague for a scholar given to self-promotion. In that glimpse I now knew his looks for future reference: instantly cast as part of myself I had never followed, who had ended up teaching in Oxford.

His identity was abruptly celebrated by explosions high into the sky. The fireworks display had caught me on the hop. Watched from the foreshore, the sparkling dissemination of light attacked the dark universe of the Solent. Puffs of

rage crackled overhead. Dying embers rained
down into anonymity. This riotous climax but not
culmination of the annual dance flashed out garish
silhouettes of the Yacht Club far to sea, the rock-
ing boats at intervals incarnadine or a sparky
green, and at each fizz and roar a racketing echo
boomed in a series of shock waves down the coast
towards Ryde.

This dazzled invalid limped home. I thought –
why me? The eternal cry of those struck down.
Why me? It now and then edged in. But of course
I knew at once when told that my trouble was serious that it was not happening to me at all. I had
disappeared. I had retired from the scene. I was
temporarily elsewhere. There was only a series of
persons into which I had broken up. They were all
over the place. They shared differing views of this
fine farce of a tragedy which healthy people mis-
called life. Being ill was the ultimate commonplace. All of a sudden it vulgarly itemized you into
sinew, ache, brain, kidney, sweat, heartbeat,
thought, muscle, habit, bone sensation – separat-
ing you into the parts you had never got together
through years of never knowing that you had to
try.

But back to that party to end parties.
In Covent Garden the celebrations fell

away, leaving only the melted ice, bottles cannon-
ing underfoot, butts of cigarettes as bitter as con-
fetti on the pavement, and an unearthly silence
down the irregularities of the lamplit street.

I waited a while. My fantasy girl had gone home.
All the rest had slipped back into their lives. For
me this was the end of something – my life of old
dispersing around me – or maybe the beginning of
more. I had nowhere to go, except a room, a flat, a
small flat, which now seemed to belong to no one.
My ego was as dark and dormant as the night. I felt
full, not of food or drink or self, but of a faraway
throb of happiness, like someone else's feeling not
yet felt. I knew I was to be triumphantly alone in
whatever I might do.

I felt I had been emptied out by the ravening wolf of the book. Did that mean it also had the
capacity to fill me again to overflowing?

Today we went to visit the coloured cliffs at Alum
Bay. Driving between the hills we cut south-west
through the inland loneliness. Beyond us sudden
precipices of chalk toppled the last of the downs
into the sea. After a greasy lunch in a pub ruined
since my last visit to Freshwater Bay, we looked at
the exterior of the hotel at Farringford. Tennyson's old home converted into the middle-class
comfort his verses offered until you caught the

pain at the back of their throat — and that was as far as I wanted to go down that tangle of lanes diminishing towards the Needles.

Was this foresight, do you think? You knew my convalescent temper was short. Any annoyance panicked out of the skin into a sweat. And just round the corner, sure enough, traffic was jammed in a lane lined with bungalows since I last saw it when rural, two coaches swollen with sightseers trying to pass on a blind corner in the heat. We backed away. After passing a chapel we emerged at speed with a whoosh of triumph on the lesser road to Alum Bay, almost got there; then slowed to a further standstill.

An amusement park hove into view. Trees parted to reveal burger saloons. Ice-cream stalls dotted acres of bus-park. Coaches shone hard in the sun. Under my collar the heat wettened blimpishly. All at once survival, or rather surviving the moment, was the issue which out of all proportion mattered.

We drove back up the hill to a turn that advertised a view of the Needles. I worried about taking it with no idea why; the road bumpy, overhangs of vegetation scratched at the bodywork. But then we came out high up on the cliffs. Far down — below the immediate surrounds, annuals of many colours tumbling out of beds, rustic furniture on the slope – lay at our feet the Needles pursuing their distant drama with the sea. There too above them loomed the downs, a serene spread of green curving across a sky daubed blue. We sat down in the open and ordered ice cream. To the west I took in the hazed view of the not quite visible Bournemouth of childhood holidays. Further south my glance just caught an outline of the Purbeck Hills which centuries ago had disgorged their marble to support the cathedrals of the years I sang treble in choirs to organs of magnitude. It was all familiar and in a slight way disengaged. There was more loss than usual in the transience of the beauty.

A view to end views.

Then I looked round and behind me saw a cottage. I did not recognize it. In the car I had told the children that years ago I had spent a holiday in a cottage close to Alum Bay. But that Victorian cottage with a tiny tower had stood alone. There had been no bungalow restaurant from which a waitress was now bringing out fried fish on a tray for a party of late lunchers; no car parks cleared out of the undergrowth: no present. And this was the moment the long-delayed shock picked on to tell me that I was ill.

I realized my memory had been shot away. That, just that, without logic, was the measure of my condition. For this of course was that same cot-

tage, dated 1868 on the keystone, with a surround
of garden, path winding down to the sea through
gorse, neck-breaking glimpse of the coloured
cliffs. Terror grabbed me. I was hemmed in by
people asserting their right to the present; taking
it casually; selecting at leisure from a menu of wide
choice. Yet my own present, long dispersed, had
been in this very spot, before the developments hit
it. I had sat here alone, drink in hand, storing up
raw material to forget.

The place was now a blank. At other tables teeth
sank into the succulence of well-fried cod. I kept
staring at the eloquence of downland descending
to the blunt exclamations of the Needles; I seemed
to be expecting them to deliver a message far beyond their capacity. I was unlikely to be told anything in the little time left. I had been brought to
this fatal pass by memory, defectible memory: the
blank I had made of a life that at the time of living
it had always felt full to overflowing.

Feeling sick for once, tired, hardly wanting to
recover, I allowed myself to be driven back to Seaview with a defiant sense that soon I must start getting my story in order.

Chapter Four

The next day, at the height of summer, *The Little Book* was published. It came out at the start of a long and humid week.

A review or two sluggishly appeared. They displayed a bitterly judicial tact, as though edging customers away from a product that might trouble them. They juggled uninspired guesses as to the identity of the author. By declaring that the book took no time to read they gave a reader the idea that he had already read it.

The volume looked tempting enough and felt good in the hand. The cover had a chequered sheen, as seductive as make-up, as warming as the sea in summer, as staunch as a favourite beer. The title appeared in small white print on the chessboard of the jacket.

The book was also tempting in price. It cost roughly the equivalent of half a seat in a back row at the opera or ten ounces of smoked salmon from Harvey Nichols or a hundred cigarettes of a low-tar brand or a sixth of a snack for two at the Ivy or

51

almost half a minute in bed with a good-class tart: a tenner less a penny.

But the weather was very hot. The country sweated it out. You could only drink and eat and listen to music and go to bed. And the heat intensified all week. And people melted, cursed, dripped, mopped and dozed their way to other places, their engines boiling as they breathed the stunned air, towards beach parks and park benches, to lakes and lay-bys, as if trying to escape their bodies that burned and peeled, sweat pouring acidly over the eyes of a fleeing nation, blinding everyone to 'a secret of life' (*Observer*), if such it was, 'modes of feeling' (*Sunday Telegraph*), if such they were.

The book had everything on paper, it seemed; but not much in fact. It slipped through the fingers. And hit the floor.

It would take time.

For the weather was altogether too hot for an event of any magnitude to matter. In such heat a war would have passed unnoticed until we were killed in the crossfire. A sticky peace prevailed. No gossip column regarded the author as being of sufficient bite to invent stories about him, no television show scooped any other, no minor scandal was fomented in the hollows of public relations. A sluggish, bitter, humid and troubling silence fell on *The Little Book*.

Except among one or two people I thought I knew, who had departed alone from the launching party, with a free copy of the book slipped into pocket or handbag, intending to read it as soon as they came home from the opera or a session with a girl, or finished dinner, smoked a cigarette or let the champagne clear from their minds. One of whom was Latimer Johns, MP for the Isle of Wight.

This evening in plush August weather we drove south to my first invitation since coming out of hospital.

A good friend, who had visited me in St Thomas's, was staying a night or two in a hotel where Dickens had started a novel close to Swinburne's house. We followed the ins and outs of the coastline, down into Sandown, up through Shanklin, last century's suburbs packed with latterday crowds sloping off towards high tea or low pub, the sunset ebbing off the land and bronzing the sea far out, before we dropped into the hidden depth of Bonchurch, where society was waiting to welcome me back in.

What would the first social occasion focused on my old life, my own life, be like? My mind floated on nerves. This friend had last seen me in a state when all friends were unreal, no part of what was really happening. I gazed at the facade of the hotel as though looking into a different century.

Over the whisky my friend seemed at a remove. We all chatted with careful indifference. I was a guest to be handled with a pity which an invalid could hardly tell from scorn. An illusion, no doubt – the result of hanging halfway in my mind between more than one life: the illness which the Island was placidly curing; the inward story of *The Little Book* that was restoring my energies; normality beckoning me with an arthritic finger back to old days. Over dinner I seemed to be talking in someone else's voice over a chasm of napery in a half-light that faded as I stared. The plates thickened with sombre gravies. Vegetables steamed obscurely in silver dishes. The wines grew heavier with every glass. Triple cream bulged over desserts. And all the while people flickered in and out of reality in the candlelight, conversation dripping as slowly as wax. I had nothing to say; even my larynx was huskily off key. Elsewhere in the ever diminishing light lurked parties of others, turning their backs on me.

I saw that in one such party sat a noted politician obviously down for the weekend at his farmhouse. Out of the corner of an eye I recognized his rear view. The balding head was bent over, absorbed in the business of cutting into a chop. If I strained my ears I could catch his drily penetrating tones, sounding a bit like myself in good form. I must have guessed aloud that he was the member for this very constituency, only to be told that in fact he was a local builder who had made a fortune out of renewing old properties by the sea. All the same he stuck in my mind. From the set of his shoulders, the thin hand lifting his glass, I felt certain I knew him. Only a glimpse, but it held my interest. How they would pity me if I insisted it was Latimer Johns MP.

Otherwise the evening went on fashioning instant art from the raw materials of an evening out. A waiter's head loomed off the ceiling over me. A huge hand grasped the neck of a gurgling bottle close to my ear. The tablecloth had a yellowish pallor, the silver glittered lethally. Caught in the grip of a slow ritual, I might have been in a church, hemmed in by discreet whispers of prayer, the baskets of bread hurrying past, the wine poured in gulps into the glasses, the chalice raised to the lips, the bread broken. The windows that had been briefly stained with sunset were now blackened by an evil gloom. The faces around me, if not quite gargoyles, had the indistinct air of visages on a reredos far above my head. Was I about to need help? I could just see how a man in a mediaeval church might be struck down by self-inflicted thoughts of mercy or damnation. I also felt, in this cathedral of solemn refreshment, that I was being denied the sacrament of real life as recommended for adults.

The MP, or local builder, or fantasy, laid down his napkin and, with a curt overall smile in everyone's direction, vanished.

I had known Latimer Johns MP at university, a young man hoping for the best. I could still see his features when I shaved in the mirror. They were there in my face, all thin: thin eyes, thinner nose, thinning hair; the bitterness tensing in the sinews of middle age, blood vessels breaking on each pinched side of the nose, eyes thinly closing against the world, on the only day that whole summer when it rained.

In Smith Square, Westminster, murmurs of domestic service set up an imitation silence within the house and *The Little Book* lay ready on a table. Breakfast waited on a warmer in more than one savoury choice. An egg slid on to his plate, velvety coffee poured into his cup. The newspapers, folded in order of priority, were skimmed in the reverse sequence.

Distant telephones purred. A skirt swished close to him, a hand placed a typed schedule on the polish of the mahogany. The day was marked out comfortably in stressed half-hours. As usual Johns realized that nothing would be made hard for him except the honed edge of loneliness that hid a knife.

A noiseless car awaited him. A cap saluted. His mind uneasily at rest he made a royal progress up the Mall to the Ministry where his desk was clear. Men came, men talked awhile, men went: the Civil Service swaying through his solitude with a tight smile. A cup of coffee was placed at his elbow. Files were passed from one tray to the next, his brain ticking over, memorizing detail. Gaps of time yawned.

Johns was to lunch officially at a Town Hall on the edge of London. A mayor swayed towards him, hand out, chain dangling, smile set. They sat down. At his elbow stood an array of glassware. Soup was placed in front of him by unseen hands. Other foods followed. He picked and sipped.

Someone stood, tapping a glass, to introduce Latimer Johns MP, who needed no introduction. Who was he? He found he was on his feet with a smile that felt denuded, facing faces. He looked at his typed papers. He began. He heard his own magnified voice touched with a regret for some ill-specified glory that had not yet occurred. He ended his speech with a sad flourish.

A hand under his elbow led him away. A face under a cap looked at a watch. His home in Smith Square noiselessly approached. A murmur of service filled the house with nothing, his only boy was away at school, his wife was nowhere, a tree clothed in acid green caught his eye from a window. There was half an hour to spare on the typed schedule.

He sat down and sighed in one of several deep armchairs poised at immoveable intervals like sleepers in a club and, as planned, picked up the small book someone had recommended him to read.

It drizzled on. The leaves were wide open in the square. Life murmured like rain below stairs where they were preparing his tea. A footman passed once in and out of the spaces of the room as unnervingly as silence. Johns had paid for it all. It was a heavy charge on him. He turned the pages of the book. In one hand, between his motionless fingers, a pencil lay ready to comment. The margins were blank. The prose opened and closed in front of his eyes, urgently echoing rain. The sounds of life, the rhythms below, grew louder, then faded into silence as a paragraph ended.

It drizzled on. He turned a page.

And now the breeze of the language was taking his breath away. The sluggish room grew cold to the touch, a hand placed hot tea at his elbow, and the argument moved forward in his mind with the elegance of a dream; whole speeches burst like fireworks in a phrase, then died into the darkness, the tea tasting deep and strong. And in the belly of the afternoon arose from the depths of the book a strong sense that this moment, unlike all other moments, would go on for ever. There was so much more to unearth in its seam of silence.

He would have to say that to someone, to his son, to friends, to many people, to the entire nation. But how? And in what language?

At this point a well-known journalist, to interview him by appointment, was shown in by a servant. Hugh Dickinson took a seat and opened his notepad; they had been at Oxford together. Johns sighed, held the book with his thumb halfway through and looked at the intruder. Who already seemed to belong to another life, to ignorance, folly and the past. 'You have to read this,' Johns found himself saying. 'It's about misery.'

'I've read it,' Dickinson said. 'I think I know what you mean. But what misery's that exactly?'

'The misery of your success,' Johns said. 'You know, it's not sweet and it's not sufficient, is it? And the misery of happiness – it doesn't live up to what you were taught to expect of it, does it? And the misery of knowing in your guts that what you're doing day after day isn't just trivial, that's a trivial point, but is also killing you. And the over-all misery you never understand, let alone conquer, because you can't find any good reason for its being there, which indeed it isn't, except that you're convinced by your anxiety that it is – am I right? And also the real misery – grief, yes, the grief at the passage of time, the egomaniac grief for others dying, yes, but most of all because you're scared that you died years ago without snatching the chance to live, aren't you? And finally the hopeless misery of having to have things you have to look after, such as lawn mowers, drawing rooms, ambitions, season tickets, watches, conceits, vehicles, selves, suitcases, radios, ornaments, vanities, illusions, weekend cottages, and all the things you're using to prevent your moving an inch, except to take out yet another insurance for a future that promises only more of the same – right?' Johns paused. 'So you'd better read it again, hadn't you?'

Dickinson stared. 'You're in great form, Minister,' he said. 'I do so very much feel bound to agree.'

Johns stood up, cast a look of visionary scorn at the journalist and made his exit obtrusive. Walking downstairs past the murmur of servants, still holding the book, he unlocked the security gate, then pulled and pushed at the garden door. It had not been opened since last summer. A lock had rusted, the bolt was stuck. He felt unable to breathe in his own house. With a kick the door suddenly gave.

Air.

Outside was a small paved garden. It belonged to him. He had slept above it for months. He had failed to visit it. He had failed even a small London garden, walled in old brick, enclosing vicarages of long ago, planted with old-fashioned roses that brought his courtship back to him. Damp lichen on the paving suggested being alone in childhood, herbs tenaciously bunching out of the crevices, a cherry tree now past flowering, recalled his father. Left for so many months to its private devices of growth, the garden seemed to mirror in sad green negative the long ignored dilemma of his heart and brain.

These problems were at once quite clear: dilemma of a politician not quite on course, not growing, getting nowhere; of a family that existed only on the paper of a daily reality that was not real; of a country that had not only stopped but gone into reverse; of a civilization that was making a public show of dispersal and defeat at just the moment of having nothing private to say.

He stood walled by the garden, stock still, discovery passing down his body like temperature rising by degrees, seeing crisply in himself the image of a man walled up in crumbling brick, planted with old-fashioned thoughts that brought nothing back to him, with damp perception clinging mossily to the lining of his brain, prejudices bunching tenaciously out of the hollows of himself, aggressions fast flowering: a thin man amid the slim chances of middle age, having had enough of life to last a lifetime, but at the same moment feeling the whole country rising in a quiet revolution behind him, as the voice of *The Little Book*, his own voice, echoed out over the miserable counties and swept him at last to power.

My love, you recognize by now the surprise of it. As I read *The Little Book* I can't help but enter into the persons of these people who are also reading it. I know how they are feeling. I am just as strongly there in Hugh's soft countryside or the metropolitan privilege of Latimer Johns as here in our own place with the text on my knee.

You can argue that this is because I have invented them, as per author's instructions. But that's not the only truth, I fear. A further likelihood is that they were there all the time, hidden in the interstices of the past. They just notched back into the present at that party launching the book.

Yes, here at last was supernature staring me in

the eye: a presence convincing me that I would soon begin to communicate with myself, in a manner that was to make the pen as crudely ancient a weapon as the sword. *The Little Book*, while perforce using the desiccated academy of words we all shared, made its real points by what it never dreamed of explicitly saying.

Thus I kept shivering as I read. The excitement made gooseflesh of time and place. On to the blank page of my mind crept the feelings of other people still very much alive. I was undergoing the convulsive pleasure of giving birth, just as you might be in the throes of creating me for yourself, darling, by the mere fact of reaching the end of this paragraph.

It took me a little time to locate the clue to all this. Who, I wondered, was Hugh Dickinson? All right, I had known him years ago, but who was he really? Nor would Latimer Johns be anyone I would particularly care to meet these days, but now he was rising out of the voluntary pages to obsess me.

And then of course I saw transparently what I had known all along: they were me, an ungrammatical me. Not as I am in any blatant sense, but as I might have been if I had chanced my arm in other walks or allowed this or that influence at various moments of the past to come uppermost. I might indeed have become a literary editor tired of his trade or a government minister searching for spicier opportunity: shadowy parallels for years building up their waste inside me, a constipation of alternatives.

But I might also have grown up to be any of those others I so despised at that party in Covent Garden which had sprung to life from all the old bashes of a lifetime. I saw unfulfilled scraps of myself, for instance, in Professor House endlessly repeating history within the honeyed warren of an Oxford college; in Sir Davis Fielden living a tradition of anxious ease on his estate; in that gloomy foreman Parry packing books for his wages but longing for his native hearth and hill in Wales; and even in Davina Darley, fantasy of a woman frolicking within me.

I knew at once that this was no literary schizophrenia; that too would spell sickness as inescapable as cancer. Instead I saw this division of the self, from which we all more or less suffered in unwitting or unwilling ways, as health, a great chorus of health. Jekyll was never just Hyde; that author's drama pictured the normal getting out of hand, the extremes at which chaps had to be pitied and straitjacketed. As for these actual characters of whom I was thinking, the several me, they were never invented out of nowhere. I was always glimpsing them in or around Seaview. They were real men and women out there, projections of me, occupying positions I might easily have filled, given not the dice falling differently but my will deciding otherwise.

In a good sense, therefore, I had done, and was doing, these things I might have done, and by believing that fiction to be true I added immensely to myself; I expanded, I breathed deeper, I put myself in a position unreachable if I had stuck out for just one self, one set of achievements, one sort of failure. Even lying in bed I enriched myself immeasurably by bringing into daily play the other people I might have been, jobs taken, things done.

Yet here I sensed a worry. The worry of being taken over by the attitudes of these people, as they started upending their lives by reading the book. All I truly wanted was to be a single and simple and growing self. But I had a suspicion that the book was urging me to get rid of them all — even as they themselves became different people as a result of digesting its content. They too, after all, had a right to strive towards new versions of things. They were as temporarily human as I was.

I asked myself: was I falling in love with Davina, as with the book that was biting deeper into me, as with the world that was coming stupendously alive? She was naked bedrooms. She was the late-night call that said the lot, the edgy promise of meeting in heart-rending places the world over. She held tight in her womb that child who would be our complicated handclasp with the future; she lay across my body for that snooze after the heavy lunch; she was the act of purring to the ends of the earth in sleeping-cars with the undercurrent of the wheels making nightly love to our ears on the narrow bunk; she was the cross-country walk that made us stumble into pubs in quest of beer, bread, cheese; she splashed me with curves of iridescent spray in that swim off the Isle of Wight; she drove me mad through Wales; she was easing fish off the grill to serve me; she was wine sipped in my arms. At last, yes, she was a country, this feminine creature growing in me, the continent I always expected of a woman but never found, as anonymous as the author, as mysterious as the book, as warming as the cold wine. All things, to one man, for ever. The woman who equalled myself.

Was myself.

And you.

Beloved, it is a shock to meet at last the woman you want, particularly if you suspect her to be a part of your own being, far too theoretical to constitute an infidelity, conceived in the heart's womb by the suddenly sexual acclaim for life that swelled in the unseen organs of *The Little Book*. It is also

wonderful to meet her, but the fact that it was unlikely to last was not, alas, an issue embraced by
the book. As far as I could see.

Now and then on the Island I did catch an abrupt
glimpse of life narrowing ahead of me.

On a close morning we had driven in gathering
gloom to Osborne, that mausoleum within a mansion. Beneath its many roofs Victoria's main duty
had been gloriously to die. It was a bank holiday.
People in a mood of ultimate patience queued almost at a standstill in the shuffle from one saloon
of state to the yet more mournful next. On all
sides I was faced with artefacts of chill marble and
paint dulled by the retreat of chic. Time curled its
toes, the brain clouded, inaction set in. I looked
hard at dead things. An ugly ego reared in me.

As we dragged into yet another unmoving room
in which Victoria had progressed towards death, I
saw my son squatting in a fidget at floor level by a
half-moon window that opened on to a garden view
of the nineteenth century. He stared out through
bars at that breathing space, a courtyard with
fountains and a stretch of cypresses standing
guard over trimmed lawn beyond; and looked like
a prisoner. I needed no further hint. Using my
stick to ruthless advantage, playing the cripple, I
shouldered my way out into the clammy liberty of

the morning where I could stroll unhindered, and not think.

These were good gardens. They enjoyed extent. Trees stood at proper intervals, singly close to, bunched at a distance. They processed masses of air.

Air.

I dosed myself on deep breaths of resin and verdancy. I watched my son playing, making mischief, released into this magnificent relic of a garden. His shouts bounced off trunks of old cedars. He kicked up divots of good lawn. His happiness and liberty roared inside my head.

The freedom to start being free.

I ask you, what would I have been like if my Victorian forefathers had failed to break out of their class? Sometimes my feet are still in the old mine, my hands quarry slate. I now remembered Owen Parry, packer and handyman at the publishers of *The Little Book*, haunting the shadows of that party, pouring drinks for his betters. I had always felt at one with his lack of luck.

He never read a word until after television of an evening and then not often, so had kept the volume by his bed for some days. At work he had overheard gossip about it. As he packed stock and the sales failed to mount in those summer weeks, he felt a loyal obligation to look it through.

He saw eye to eye with failure. He liked a romance.

One night after some warmed-up steak and kidney pie, a couple of cups of tea and an hour of the box, Parry placed the book on his knee and opened it with tentative fingers. His glasses blinked over several pages. There seemed somewhere to be a story in them, but it kept fading like eyesight: something about a rural mansion, stunned by luxury, a slim dark twit of a newspaperman who had fallen in love, a politician trying to change the country if not the world with some wordy panacea which he wittily summarized at candlelit dinners attended by lady mucks, an aristocratic villain unfaithful to his wife, bending a rosy-cheeked maidservant across his knee and beating her . . .

Had Parry nodded off? Well, he had dozed and, while pretending to read, dreamed. He recalled from the story a scintillating atmosphere that somehow excluded him, yet could put his finger on no detail. Several incidents seemed to have slipped past, as though to avoid him. He tried to see how it all hung together, but felt bothered by the effort.

A read to end reads.

Yet when he looked back over the pages of his life the whole book was distastefully familiar. He had surely lived through this story, suffered with the nit of a hero whoever he was, fallen for the heroine who had flirted into the action just the once. Outside his window a bawdy racket lingered in the sadness of the pubs, drunks scattering like memories into the sodium-lit void of the Lambeth night. Lorries on the main road were already pounding towards the markets with tomorrow's vegetables and fish. Life went jaggedly on mystifying his poor brains. His late wife had been a cut above him, a bit of a lady. He thought he had loved her but now he was alone.

Alone with a book.

Parry raised his eyes from the text. Unexpectedly, with the force of fact, it struck him that he had lived quite alone throughout his life, ever since as a boy he left home, that dilapidated democracy of work and song on the far edge of Wales. The book had touched his origins. It evanescently reminded him, as romances did, that ever since his roots withered he had lacked some element that now seemed the best of life.

The narrative had done its best to catch him, he thought, but wasn't it too late? One page after another was straining to carry him off into the future; here, however, he sat at a standstill, the words twisting a knife so bluntly in his dormant emotions that someone else seemed to be having those feelings on his behalf. And he kept knowing that the next sentence would by a miracle explain not only the plot, but the bitter dream that hit him when he dozed over the book, the reason for packing books all day to earn a living, the nocturnal haste of the lorries and the cries of the drunks, the inner obtuse silence stretching back over half a century. Parry awaited the moment in the story when all the ranting statesmen, toffs who fancied maids, literary gents saying the wrong thing and women in muddles even worse, took all the threats in their stride, behaved like their own true selves, fell into one another's arms, and changed for the better with their clothes on.

This did not seem to be happening. Wondering what naked secret the last page would hold, Parry fell asleep in his chair as if waiting up for someone.

The Little Book dropped off his knee.

And lay on the carpet face down.

Waking up in Seaview, twisted into my pyjamas, I disliked having to spell these other selves out for myself. It seemed, as soon as thought of, so obvious. Yet not only had I no need to tell anyone else about it – the inhabitants of Seaview whose looks had filled a vacancy or two, people walking dogs on the beach, the trippers galore – but I could see no sign that anybody else – politicians strutting across the face of the papers, moguls of the box dictating what our world might or must see of ourselves, psychiatrists skidding over the thin ice of the unconscious, scholars digging their own graves in fields no longer worth excavating – had any such simple sense of the obvious as I had.

Was it purely because I was dying that I wanted a moratorium put on ways of life that were not up to much?

No, it was for the angrier reason that by now I knew I was not dying.

Every day and in every way I felt better. And better. The scar cast off its crust. The abdomen lolloped back into order. The legs took to walking. The neck held itself poised and painless. The midriff distended under the fattening benevolence of food and drink. The brain held fast to the unexpected luxury of a span of time in which it could spread its wings. As the strength grew I formed a certainty, or had a shrewd idea, or was lulled by the seaside into a suspicion, or accepted from a general sense around me of all going well, that I was not dying.

I was not dying. Here I was putting on weight. You were looking after me. Here I was growing up. You were helping me. Here I was arguing the toss.

I looked you full in the eye. How could I or anyone else be dying?

Chapter Five

One of our neighbours on the Isle of Wight was a tall bespectacled figure of my age to whom I had never spoken. He had a remotely aristocratic air. I had noted with sympathetic envy his habit of observing the boats through a telescope mounted on a tripod. His lawn was immaculate. His flowers were trim and healthy in their beds. His house had been unnaturally still this past week.

Someone then told me he had a cancerous kidney that had become inoperable, perhaps from late diagnosis.

For days I felt very much at one with a stranger. I was divided from his reflections only by a creosoted fence: wishing I had known him, sorrowing that his lease of life was to be short, glad that by the luck of my night of pain I had not been so condemned, feeling in this similar house that close at hand I had a friend on whom I could never call.

I supposed him to have been mostly in bed this month, for last night I learned that tomorrow he was to make his possibly final exit, at least from the Isle of Wight. He was being taken – by island roads, by ferry, by the highways I knew from childhood – to the King Edward VII Hospital in London and I felt anxious to be here when he left. I wished to witness such a departure, to share with him last glimpses, to rehearse.

That evening I gazed out on strong grey drizzle that for once hid the mainland and wondered if his eyes were on the boats bobbing in the washed-out weather and hoping they were. His example prepared me for my own exit; it made death companionable.

I would wish of myself, aware of the risk of soppiness in any such urge, the silence I considered particularly his. I wanted this curious foretaste he gave me, this sense of leaving the much-loved, as I voyeured across the fence: a room low lit upstairs, a grey-haired lady below it glued to the television set in distress, roses rambling in a wet garden. It came to me how agonizing it was in life ever to think how little time was directly spent on living.

Next morning just before eight, when under high cloud I was off to get the papers, the ambulance was drawn up in the street. I stood a moment in guilt, retracing a step or two. To eavesdrop, to spy. Through the roses tangling the fence I saw the patient, at least his head, emerge from the front door, hunched in a chair, some easing words spoken: a vision of terminal ordinariness that haunted me all the way up to the shop, for the milk and croissants, and beyond. I thought I knew just what I might feel if I were not dead when carried on a last journey: things one might register from the corner of an eye obsessed by survival, swathes of buddleia and isolated plums hanging over the neighbour's fence, shrubs I might have planted decades ago, a sense of a lifelong Seaview waking up, going to fetch its bread and milk and news, knowing I would never do it again, never again; possibly not minding that finality, if the inconvenience of pain or of staying alive were too much for me, not to mention the corollary: being inconvenient to others with every breath I gainlessly drew. And then there was sudden noise looming down the street, the day's first open-topped bus to Ryde, a woman's hair on the upper deck breezed in a sudden burst of sun, rounding the corner. And by then my neighbour had gone.

Looking out to sea later, still stricken by a sense of loss, a loss pointed by the reiterative slosh of the waves, I was called over to light the barbecue. We were to lunch at the table between the hydrangeas overlooking the sea. On the grill the chops sizzled. Potatoes broke open with a gush of steam. Eating solemnly, thinking of next door's emptiness, overborne by the open-air disorder of the children who might all too soon be fatherless, I wondered whether it was now too late to start again, if not on the search for a new personality easier for me or anyone else to live with, at least on a project that did not repeat my past.

It would be quite a plunge to start again. Meanwhile this potato needed more pepper.

Drinking the 1989 Adgestone, I savoured the idea of a fresh start: an impulse infuriatingly associated with youth, even extreme youth. I refilled my glass while slipping more butter into my potato. I was old. The sun shone.

I emptied my glass and concentrated. At my age, and in my shape, the only extension of life to which you were entitled was to kick yourself out of your rut. This was just what the operation could do for me. I could, and must, expel myself from my past, by virtue of the plain fact that I had no future. That gave me a present.

I refilled my glass, this time with Chinon, favourite of Rabelais, bought up the road.

The long afternoon overheated. I moved indoors for a rest thinking of you, my love, outside. You see me through. You see through me. I never see our joint past as past, only my solo one that lasted the half-century before we met. That's past, but ungot rid of. You are a continuous present, giving birth daily to future. Remind me to tell you this – though you will not care for the taint of high-flown banality. Especially halfway through the summer holiday. Sorry, I'm beginning to doze off . . .

And sense the dangers in the book. On various pages that darkened in my mind I detected a hint of evil.

For one thing: all these impulses to change my life were running away with me. I was being forced back by this little drug – itself both a book and a discipline – to the virginal moment before I learnt any discipline or read a single book.

The wily volume sought to be my only good. It had no patience with the cultured half-measures that populated my life. It evoked in me a lust for a clean return to the primitive. Picking on the old adolescent training that still blinkered my vision, it tried to expel the odours of classroom dust, textbooks with torn spines, that world in which influential penumbrae of old men were for ever creating simulacra of young ones in school or college – the remnants of a tried system which for centuries had been making me the mix of the man I was.

In fact the book put me squarely back at the university. My friend Professor D. J. House was now standing on the rostrum, hair disordered, hunched in a vulturial gown. With a disrupted look at his students he opened a slim volume. It was not the oldest poem in English, on which he was billed to lecture, but the newest prose. He had spent half the night reading *The Little Book*.

The professor introduced the text with his usual wittily ambiguous preamble. He read aloud from it just as he might intone the lesson in chapel, except that increasingly he appeared to be disowning the gospel. He sneered at these glimpses of novelty. He seemed to detest the threats to social order and personal calm alike that pulsed in the words. His lip curled.

But his students rallied out of their habitual tedium. They listened, words chopping sideways into their brains, phrases cutting. Beyond the latticed blanks of the windows that let in so little light, fanfares of traffic rolled in echo down the Oxford streets as Professor House held up the book to arcane ridicule.

And at last stood down. Tense with scorn he strutted home to a luncheon party in honour of old varsity contemporaries, a junior minister, a noted journalist, landed gentry on the decline. They were well into their cups by the coffee.

Meanwhile the students marched off to the bookshops where they dispersed among the stacks, slipping *The Little Book* criminally into canvas bags stamped with flags or slogans. Within minutes they emerged, flicking pages, breaking into quotes, forming gangs under the climbing roses in a spring tide of protest, lecture halls dropping into the stony past, familiar walls of colleges vanishing in a hail of catchphrases, until they arrived amid cricket at a crucial moment in the game: a green sward as long and wide as summer dotted at rhythmic intervals by figures crouched in intense white as if waiting for the truth to thud into their hands.

The newcomers flopped down and stared against the sun into the pages of the book. For a while a cryptic silence fell. And then all round the field, in a mutter that rose and fell with the scatter of clapping at the slap of a boundary, conversations began trying to make not sense but capital out of the words. At first these exchanges seemed to be citing a manifesto. In the heat of the moment propaganda yawned. But then the tone subtly changed: the book had to be translated into higher terms, made flesh and rounded out, fulfilled in action. *The Little Book* had to be theirs.

Yet the book had already been twisted out of true by a professor. He had patronized it. He had widened a generation gap by attempting to narrow the text down to sense, by feeding them with chunks as indigestibly out of context as their syllabus. Here were solid grounds for protest. They must march – march to ensure that never again would *The Little Book* be failed – march to expose that teacher as a reactionary – march to purge the renegade. *The Little Book* was all theirs. It set the standards which their youth gave them the right to impose on everyone. They should be ready to kill or die for it.

I then knew, as clearly as if dreaming it, that Professor House was to be murdered. I felt him calling for help inside me. But also I knew he was not real. He was an old unfocused part of myself. No doubt it was high time he was taken out.

The perils of the book struck me anew. In the desperation of my mind's eye I could see the professor walking away from me, miles away, down a narrow mediaeval street of shadows with the last of the sun glinting off attic windows. He was entering a college that seemed at first sight deserted. He came upon the scene of a dress rehearsal. It was an open-air production of *Julius Caesar* against a senate of massed roses on the college lawns. The high walls were hung with drapes of late clematis in the dusk. From afar a group of male students, attired in a conspiracy of white robes as luminous as the flowers, loomed towards him over the soundless turf in a half-circle. It was clear that the treachery in that far-off Roman dawn was about to be enacted in this English twilight. For their eyes were poised on hatred, a hatred born somewhere in the bilious maw of *The Little Book*.

'I did not mean what I said,' the professor cried.

Then saw mesmerized a rush of roses swollen on the eye, walls at angles, traditions cracking, felt for a second agonizingly intent upon the unresolved ramifications of his life, when the first blow from the half-moon of conspirators struck him like a farcical explosion of dentistry in his mouth, and then he was on his back, dreading more pain, and a knife, not made of rubber, entered at speed his lower belly, and Caesar's blood spilt and gurgled on to the lawn, the deep purple sky woozing over him as if drunk, and he at last knew himself to be alone, denied the chance of telling the world, from the elevated podium of his values, in better language, how very crucial this little book was, how it outclassed Beowulf, the Bible, Shakespeare, Milton on the more paradisaical ground of its choice, how it struck out of a phrase the steel that might make a man, how in particular it destroyed the point of this whole declining garden wrapped in serenity at dusk; and then, the feet of his assailants tumbling past him, he thought he might be dying, soon felt a slack human damp on his waistcoat, breathed once more all the mown smells of order and propriety, then snuffed it.

Nearby, in the silence, a crocket, high on a

chapel roofline, toppled. Here and there the empty city cracked faintly, easing itself as if breathing a last deep breath. The foundations, first of a library, then of a senior common room, now of a principal's lodging, created underfoot. A cornice or two fell into the blank quads, crushing a tangle of bikes; a gargoyle bit grotesquely into well-tended grass. Books stored underground loosened their support of the tons of masonry above them in that long instant before the assembled colleges flopped down at all angles into explosions of stone, overwhelming scholars in their panelled lives, burying the past in the past. Thus in a matter of moments buildings that had stood firm for centuries in that city centre, the heart of a world, had reverted to the chaos of their raw materials. A hundred acres of age-old thought were lying at last in their own ruins, while the dust of which they had always been composed settled over the magnificent defunction in a pall that might be seen for miles or years.

As I breathed out of my nostrils the last of that inner dust I knew that all this activity, subtly urged by *The Little Book*, had been happening in the unnoticed shallows of myself. Over the years I had created that professor, indeed that city, out of the wrong areas in me, where the nerve to be someone other than myself twitched under the skin. Now I had taken the chance to destroy one at least of the malformed people who were preventing my growth into the only kind of person I might respect: as positively simple as a manifesto, as decent as a game of cricket, as unambiguous as an act of love, as primitive as boys let loose in a garden. In the light of *The Little Book*, which had ranged all over the continent – in the thick of Marseilles, darling, the environs of Rome, Lisbon's heart – for answers, depths, changes, it was hardly asking much to be that one straight person.

Anything less than a generous response to the book's generosity was suicide.

Twice a day, swirling on to the choppy arena beyond the foot of my bed, appeared the Seaview dinghies watercoloured in their strips and wedges of shimmeringly bright sail, racing, glissading, all set to win: a scene riveting once I knew which buoys were the aim of their aggressive tacking. And soon the boats became people as I recognized one by one the known solitaries who in unlikely clothes dashed out of the bigger houses or down from retreats inland to scull out a bit late to their vessels about to compete: always a race against time, invariably at the mercy of variables.

I walked out this morning for the papers via the back street, Rope Walk, where a high-walled tiny

garden supported thick-stemmed sunflowers rising to the villa's roofline. On the return journey,
stick tapping down the more public street, I
paused on the High Street corner to look at the
formal list in the glass-fronted case which named
the ships, many of note and tonnage, which would
pass either way by day or night over the next week,
a timetable more reliable than my own. I glanced
dryly at the agreeable exclusion practised by the
Yacht Club in their waterside yard, my envy
heightened by the discovery that temporary mem-
bership cost fifty pounds a week. But the higgledy-
piggledy structure, narrow passages and odd
levels, was at the crux of Seaview, as if the town
behind existed merely to supply it with both purpose and personnel. Everything of interest happened out to sea. Everyone's focus was on the local
brand of infinity.

My own haunt was the Seaview Hotel, a hundred
yards back from shoreline activity. In the front bar
the walls were hung with framed ships, from the
first Cunarder of 1840 at its top-hatted launch to
(avoiding the *Titanic*) the monumental liners of
our mid-century now junked. I drank my pint of
beer as if actually embarked on one such scrapped
marvel. The bar I sat in, busy but never crowded,
seemed to be perpetually travelling elsewhere

through the calm weather enjoyed by all the photographs.

To fall sick was to join a club more exclusive and ultimately more expensive than the Sea View Yacht Club. On the phone I spoke this evening to two friends of roughly my age who had both just been ill, one struck by a brain haemorrhage but now sounding sprightly, the other in and out of trouble with her oesophagus and speaking along the wire in a withdrawn voice. We were all people productive but put at question, about to spend too much of what remained of our lives in therapy or hospital or dying, holding in common a passport to nowhere much. We were eager to meet because of a shared understanding of time's littleness; meanwhile in a masonry of impending death we joined hands over the telephone.

I slept well and awoke keenly to the idea of the book – ah! the book. I swung off the bed. A scent and sizzle of bacon arose downstairs. I must get fully better faster. The memory of wanting to know enough about living to fashion that guide to it which the book would be, to sit back in luxury with it all tied up, to have said everything: I had never lost this desire. It did not have to be a book. Indeed now it was unlikely to be.

I lacked the energy.

A biro dropped out of my grip in seconds as the

eyes drooped, my head nodded over the typewriter, my will slipped like a drunk sideways to the floor.

But my mind could do it. Just let the imagination float and flourish! Why need I share with anyone else the excesses to which I had the key? Sit here in peace and work it out for myself. Tell my stories to an audience of one. Spout for all I was worth, preach at the sea, turn reality into dreams, enjoy my talents without subjecting them to the chill of any criticism but my own. We were no longer talking of visions that would transform the world. We were talking of enjoying ourselves to the full. Within minutes I was dressed and downstairs and everyone, plunging me into the intensive care which a perfectly good invalid was made to suffer, told me how spruce I looked.

It was not the moment to tell you that in the interstices of my mind I was fiddling around with the idea of turning my whole life into a masterpiece to which nobody would have access but yours truly.

Or you.

Chapter Six

❧

Lying in bed, almost halfway through reading *The Little Book*, during a passage stirred by an undertow of sensuality, I managed with difficulty to remember Sir Davis Fielden.

His was the lofty figure that ghosted away from me at that launching party, a sketch for whom I had glimpsed in the invalid next door in Seaview. Who had gone away to hospital. Of whom I had no news.

My own version of this baronet, as unreal as the real thing, had been forming for years inside me, an ideal of manners, courage and honour dying somewhere in rural vacuum from a seepage of purpose.

An aristocrat of sorts.

Into the vibrant air of the book he now emerged as one of its early readers.

His setting was a midsummer vision, as recalled in that first weak outing to the ruins of Appuldurcombe. A stately home packed to the doors with art. Skies shivering with birdsong. Coverts riddled with game. Borders stupid with perennials. A childish dream containing in a syrupy fold of the hills an England whose silence seemed glued to eternity, this house possessed the grandeur of scale on which my ambitions still always had more than half an eye. It represented the everlasting peace to end my war with the world, a nook where tradition and rank allowed any quiet excess, such as the seduction of a maidservant over a table in the gunroom or the formulation of a masterpiece over a decade in the library. Yes, old dreams of mine, if not of yours.

Though I had never known Sir Davis well, I felt him at this moment brooding inside me, dragging me back. All too easily I could guess his barber, his clubs, what he had done in the war. Never in my life would I attain to such style and wealth. Yet the attics of his mind were both uninhabited and in anguish.

Sir Davis began to skim *The Little Book* out of courtesy. He saw it as paying his dues. For having attended the party.

A suspicion dawned on an early page that it lacked moral stature. He tiptoed to a cupboard. He laid hands on some brown paper which he wrapped round the binding. He had an awkward sense that his 'psychic' wife was reading over his shoulder, but whenever he looked up no one was there, only a maid in black stoking the fire. (He was thin-blooded even in summer.) He kept stumbling across words which he articulated under his breath as if mouthing an improper suggestion. At length, troubled, he laid the book aside to go and consult a gardener about some bedding plants.

Lady Fielden passed through the high over-heated room on her way to an afternoon rest. And snatched up the book. One of her 'promptings' told her that it contained a message.

In the open air Sir Davis was even more perplexed. The book seemed to be fumbling among long-mislaid desires. For years he had wanted nobody. But now, since scanning those guilty pages, he saw his life pass into the hands of some libidinous assassin of his calm. While stuttering instructions to the gardener, he imagined he smelt the soft, hot wafts of a female body rising from the rosebeds. Even back in front of the smouldering fire, awaiting his tea, he felt a clumsy fist of desire closing over parts of him accustomed to neglect.

Was this deep commotion in his body tricking him – into a future which at his age, surely, he jolly well ought to have ceased to contemplate?

The maid brought in tea. In laying the things she almost stifled him with her rosy scent which he had never noticed before. She eased a black hip

close to his face as she bent low over her duties. He
glimpsed the silken cleft moulded by her skirt.

His teeth seesawed falsely into buttered toast.

His eye, following the maid's exit, vaguely
looked for the book.

God, where had he put it?

The thing was hot, secret, ignominious.

He began to tremble in the suddenly empty
room. As if a servant, a ghost, had stolen the book.
Or his conscience.

Upstairs, in a lingering fashion, Lady Fielden had
taken off all her clothes. She wrapped a silk orien-
tal drape round her body and disposed her limbs
to rest on the bed. While laying the book open on
the pillow at the first page, she briefly considered
the acute rapture of sleep. Her dreams were sean-
ces. Their knocks and hushes echoed for hours in
her ears. And the book, oh goodness: words to her
were projectiles that one aimed at servants or
males but otherwise kept in their place.

She eased her legs. These words seemed to be
quite different. They were as psychic as she. She
strained her eyes but could not quite hear what
was being said. It was as though a spectral someone were overhearing her thoughts even before
they passed through her mind. She concentrated

hard for a second. She felt herself dissolving into that other being, or person, or shade.

And at that moment, as I read, darling, I sensed myself becoming her. Or just being close to you?

Anyway I was being deeply drawn into her mood. I want to rid myself – the book was telling me – of this burden of a house. Let little men in green aprons be hired by the dozen to divest me of these clothes, those aching grounds, this excess of home. It must all be done with hushed propriety, so that I never notice it happening, all accomplished behind my back because I cannot bear to lose it: not yet, not yet.

Yes, I said these words myself, while also being aware of her voice. Yes, I had never picked out of the ether a message so clearly before; *The Little Book* had fetched it up out of the deafness of years. Yes, suddenly I had eased into being this middle-aged woman lying on her bed in a welter of dimensions, faculties, which she had always, without knowing for sure, expected to exist. In her haunted home, in the shape of ghosts. Or in her person, as perceptions.

And now I was in her skin. I knew, with the book in my hand, that someone I would normally think expendable – a withering woman reclusive in her privilege, married to a numbskull, tucked into boredom by art and breeding — was someone within me I really needed.

I had spotted her about Seaview, of course, chatting quietly on the sea-wall. Everyone knew her, the dry humorist young beyond her years, desirably trim of figure and acute in wit, refusing without fuss to consider herself old. Into my daily reflections this woman in her seventies had tumbled as a token of durability. A token of the containable shocks of whatever lay ahead. Of the discoveries available to anyone of her sprightliness, femininity and calm.

For Lady Fielden I feel a bizarre affection, as at this instant all things unnecessary to her life are poised to depart in spirit. Gone her need for yesterday's tables and chairs that only furnished illusions, for the canvases on the walls that cut her off from her own way of looking, for the marriage that for years blinded her to matters that mattered more. Here she lies on her bed in a comfort she hardly values. Nothing real around her is real any longer. The sculptures of high value they own are no more than random images in too few dimensions. The roses down there in the borders are blooming to no avail.

The thought of having lived here in daily tedium for half a century abruptly means nothing to her, indeed to us both. I experience the ecstasy of

knowing that Lady Fielden, with recourse only to
herself, not to drugs or fantasy or despair or alcohol, has been sprung by *The Little Book* into the
destruction of what she knows to be destroying her
– the paltry assumption that life, as we knew it,
was truly life, as is.

She lay in bed wondering with whom she was in
touch. This uncanny book had flushed presences
into the house: not evil, but powerful ones, perhaps devoted to her.

They seemed to want her to be happy while telling
her that she had never known happiness.

Were these ghosts rags of herself, torn sheets
spooking her corridors with comedy? No, no, the
soul of this little book had crept into her. It was
showing her the woman she had missed all these
years behind the leisured tensions that trod quietly about the house with her, the blind anxieties
that woke her to palpitations in the small hours.

But are you downstairs? On this wavelength I
long for your help. What exactly were these drift-
ing specimens of half-existent ectoplasm, or whatever you cared to call them, asking her to do . . . ?

Safer ground. In another apartment of the
doomed house, one lined with shotguns and tro-
phies of the chase, Sir Davis was hard at work. It
did not matter what he had always secretly wanted
to do. All that counted was that now on that rough

couch he was doing it. Whether he stripped the maid down or left her stockings ruckled above the knee or spread her wide or forced his way between tight thighs or splayed her loosely on top of his frame or with his fingertips touched her nipples through silk or pumped her on the stone flags or stood her fainting against a showcase or bent her over the baize of a billiard table or just plain fucked her as we all fuck; the detail did not matter. All that counted was that, his brains swimming with children he never fathered, his dicky heart beating across an ocean of pleasure and coming up with the eldorado, the rhythms tuning the extremities of his body, the impropriety cracking every mystery that had long been closed to him, in a naked gunroom, he was managing it. And the resilience of her flesh beneath him took it and responded to the last inch of it and opened up to it and rose in sound and fury to the heights of the room before subsiding with a moan to the floor, as he took her with the last-minute youth of age and she gushed out to him with the old intensity of youth. The best thing in life had happened for the one and only time.

Sir Davis buttoned up, coughed and grinned. 'That'll be all,' he said, in one of the book's solitary lines of dialogue, had he been a character rather than just a reader, 'for the moment.'

This evening at the Seaview Hotel I took my pint of bitter out on to the terrace. As kept on happening in regatta week, the local focus had shifted elsewhere. All the toffs and trippers had flocked to a tug-of-war taking place on a distant field. The result was no traffic in the High Street, bars empty, one or two solitary drinkers including myself at quiet ease outside the hotel. A relaxed young man passed with oars carried at the horizontal under his arm. Tame sparrows flitted around the white iron chairs, then flew off scared without reason into the thorned safety of old-fashioned roses. Faint sounds of infants being bathed penetrated my inner ear. All these bits and pieces of phenomena had something in common with memory.

They felt like past.

There had been this morning the drive to Adgestone along the backbone of the Island, chalk slopes brimming with summer, to buy a case of their nice wine. I was starting tentatively to feel that the Island was entering into the spirit of my recovery by seeming a place of ample habitual happiness. I had a sense of being drawn into a society to which no harm could come. Dangers were too far away to matter. They afflicted others elsewhere. Here I had slipped into the doldrums of simple pleasure. Or such was the illusion. The surgeon at St Thomas's had told me of no link between the disease he had routed out and the drinking that punctuated my days. I was taking the expert at his word. I had longed for alcohol again, to extend self-satisfaction, to exceed it. It was not I who might become dependent on it but the days that already had. As for me, my only concern was to get better.

So a glass of sherry for elevenses never came amiss, nor another at noon. Excellent beer was always on tap in the hotel where indeed I now sat drinking some of it while assessing this regime of mine. Floods of Adgestone irrigated the picnic lunches. With a need to raise some defence against thinking that life was beyond its best, I found the day's slump in mid-afternoon hardly tolerable without the kick of a fluid, say brandy. The evenings, being in limited supply, required unlimited gin and Dubonnet, not to mention a serious vintage to round off the day's recovery, whereafter a slug of whisky helped me up to bed. And I was aware throughout that the real security I was drawing from the Island came not from drink but from the past. I was feeding off not my angst but the plenitude of the nineteenth century – which had thought of itself, built itself, as eternity.

Now, tug-of-war far off, a hung calm immobilized the outer parts of this pub. In the warm air I swigged and brooded. Life occurred marginally at intervals. The rubbery murmur of a mountain bike diminished uphill. This garden where I sat, wasps grizzling in and out of the leafage, was now in shadow, only the geraniums glaring within the dusk.

I felt a very long way away from whatever man it was that I had been before my illness.

Very close to what man I might be tomorrow, if I ran out of luck.

Miles from immortality.

Two girls with arms round each other passed at a remove down the street. Aircraft, hovercraft: far murmurs of travel grumbling above, pulsing across the sea in the view ahead of me, cocooned me in silence. My chest tensed into inarticulacy, eyes gulped, mouth swam with tears. I was not likely to get out of this without a struggle, or perhaps in any case.

Beer to hand, I had to think of something else or bust, so I did the former.

From the outskirts of the party that launched *The Little Book* I recalled that tall louche figure, not unlike me in appearance, alas, who unsteadily drifted on his way into deeper Soho.

In passing he had stolen a copy with no purpose other than to flex his delinquency.

Certainly he wanted no book.

Books were the cultural equipment that had wrecked him.

Books taught him the gamut of facts he detested knowing and never needed.

But it slipped into his pocket as easily as a loaded automatic. Slick like a wad of fivers. He lurched on his way down King Street, thinking, in circles, as ever, about how to set himself free of his habits, or release himself, altogether, from the habit of living.

In forty years of applied consumption Dave Higgs had elevated the demon drink into the angel art. He rarely showed its effects. Used it to enhance his charm. Berated dinner tables of notables, for a humour shortage or a pomposity glut, in tones too loud or terms too offensive. Was often forgiven. Drinks drained his brain of shyness while sharpening his wits into malevolence. His art hid from everyone his misuse of time; the hangovers were behind blinds. He mingled with professionals who made a career of booze, politicians with as many veins broken as promises, lawyers as often under the table as under instruction. His was a crafty sobriety, an increasingly glazed mask that must soon crack. But for the moment he continued to haunt his locals, waiting for someone to surprise him into reform. Wanted, a polished lover to spring out of woodwork long rotted.

Wanted, a job to be proposed by someone less sloshed than himself. His flat was in Pimlico, his mind in turmoil, his bank account in Swansea, his penis in recoil, his spirit in retreat, his suits were in disrepair, his women despairing of his ways, his affairs in disorder. His idea of noon was a pub, his notion of midnight a bed.

This evening then.

Knees wobbly, face blank with bonhomie, after a few minutes in the French pub, slapping a shoulder, kissing a face.

Dropping in at the Academy, nobody much there, patting his pockets with a frown, a sense of something stolen, an object that was his. His own.

Take it easy, do not lose your rag or they will assume you paralytic . . .

And Dave thought back with care. He consulted the hints of the evening left in his mind, blinking in drizzle at a so-called friend in Old Compton Street who got away in a taxi, bugger, they were running off with his book: yes, it was a book.

Leaning at a bar tended by a bearded wiseacre, he now drank six oysters between blinks of sleep.

And fell to the floor.

The next time his eyes opened was in a taxi at his front door. (Five quid.) Where was he? He and the book?

Someone's theft of the book was the first point

to surface next morning in Pimlico. To his sticky gaze the day framed in the window a damp revenge. He felt robbed. His mind insulted. A question nagging.

What could be so good about a book worth pinching in a pub?

Somewhere here Higgs detected illogic, knowing of old that a drunk had no purposes, let alone morals; I just do or say things at random, your honour, on my way to stupefaction.

And with equal lack of logic, even before the morning's first drink, he started blaming the book – darkly accusing it of being stolen. Challenging it to give itself up! Or risk arrest!!

His awareness that this was a game did nothing to quell his rage at being outmanoeuvred by a mere book. First in a Pimlico pub, then on more familiar Soho ground, his voice in fits and starts leant on the bar and ranted on and rambled about the book, this little book that had cheated him, not that he had read it, sod it, but as though he had written the fucker. Men he knew with poached eyes edged away into other pissed groups. A girl's attention sagged with all this talk of the book he was looking after for a friend but had got away. He lectured a captive barman on his disappointment – with the escaping text, with pals letting you down, with, towards closing time, the effect of booze.

Aka life. The life that snatched your book, only to ignore you, laugh at you, fail to buy you drinks.

One for the road, come on. A drink to end drinks.

Whereupon a miracle occurred.

Forgetting last night's half-dozen, Higgs thought he might spend his last tenner on some oysters, a glass of wine, ending all with a flourish. Also forgetting where he had fetched up last night, he breezed into a wine bar and summoned a chap with a beard. 'Same again?' said mine host inexplicably.

A tottering memory pierced the blackout. With a wink he handed over his banknote.

While insubstantially chewing on the tangy slime of an oyster he awaited his change. Into his hand were delivered a few coins plus unbelievably a ten-pound note – by instinct at once pocketed: what good odds for drinking white wine and eating shellfish, and in the same second it struck him: that little book was priced at a penny under a tenner. Fate had awarded him a second chance. No fear of arrest now. No prison. An honest citizen, he could now go out and lavish this accidental largesse on his very own copy of the book that had been giving him trouble for days.

He beckoned the beard over.

'Where's a bookshop?' Higgs said.

A slight pause, eyes glaring.

'Oh,' cried the beard, 'so it's yours!' And in a trice he laid in front of Higgs a slightly battered copy of *The Little Book*.

With tipsy reverence Higgs picked it up. Tears bloated the corners of his eyes. One hand gripped the book as if for good. The other from his trouser pocket held out the gash tenner.

'Give me wine, landlord,' Higgs said with a sob, still eyeing the book in its chequered livery, 'and join me in a glass.' All done and said not only with an air of having discovered the paranormal, but with the intention of reading, before he died of cirrhosis, this blasted curative something of a book.

'I read it,' said the beard blandly, raising his glass. 'I read the lot. Likes to think it's written for the upper crust, but actually it's for wine-bar managers and don't let any wanker tell you different.'

Chapter Seven

꧁꧂

Dave's loss of the book clicked with the Seaview mood this late August. The emphasis was on childish things.

Children's sports took over the beaches. Eggs rolled off spoons into the sand. Boys and girls grew three-legged to zigzag over the last tide's wrack. Yachts raced back and forth in adult tomfoolery, adrenalin going for the win, the kill, the return home for pouring out champagne and gossip while the weather beat all records. The mood of Seaview in that fortnight of fun was just right for steeling me to survival. Everyone else was taking living for granted, which spurred my intention of staying alive. I liked being an inactive small part of a small society immensely busy within so small a space of time as a week.

The sports in Seagrove Bay were crisply organized. When we arrived late at ten past nine this morning the flat racing for the nines to tens was nearly over. A lady in repulsive shorts careered up and down with signs announcing age-groups,

while her gentleman alternative readied and stea-
died the line-ups on the sand before whistling
them off. I found it intimately regressive, as sepia
as a school sports day half a century ago. The
proprietor of a local hotel in blazer and whites
sauntered past, imitating Hugh Dickinson on his
best behaviour. I leaned on my stick feeling
young.

This afternoon, the esplanade packed, I
watched in a mild agony of boredom the repeti-
tions of the diving competition off the pier.

At any moment I might, or must, take off. But I
stayed, mesmerized by everyone's sheer energy.

Above the watery stage of these events the
Yacht Club had a dress-circle look while the cheer-
ing plebs were jammed in the pit outside the pub.
But the diving was nothing to the greasy pole; and
they came dressed for it, dressed for this slippery
plunge into sex, this act of cartoon lechery in full
and farcical public view: a pirate blackly winking
with his eyepatch, a couple of transvestite tarts in
fishnet stockings and overwhelming hats, a six-
foot baby with a pacifier waddling along the pole
in a nappy, now and then a willowy girl of great
beauty lighting up the spirit as she teetered, slithered, with a hilarious splash went spouting
under − into a sea soon awash with wigs, cocked
hats, sodden diapers, ostrich feathers. Equally

competitive seagulls screamed overhead in time-less lunges unnoticed by all. I eventually sneaked off for a beer.

What was right for me now here at Seaview I could put into a sentence. I liked the amiable combination of the suburban mood in which I grew up, the mystery of the maritime that always brooded in me, the snug bounds of a community various enough to be ideal for anyone's concept of a society, the sense of expanding to island size, the feel of a countryside which yards from home grew wild within the miniature terms that were the making of it, the proximity of fresh fish, the huge skies and longer views, the interweaving smells of sea-weed and lawn clippings, wine – and the ever-present faint shock of still being alive. As was, to my faint annoyance, Hugh Dickinson still alive. His routines at a standstill, he was now keeping an eye nervously on office screens and faxes for news.

At first a few isolated incidents, tapped out between rising prices and falling stocks, struck him as possibly connected with *The Little Book*. But were they coincidental? If not, what did they mean?

A market gardener near Hereford, overloaded with alimony and several children, was feeling the pinch; vegetables at market had dropped in price to a hardly appreciable degree. Was it possible that people were eating less? Somewhere on the Isle of

Wight a fisherman, just managing to keep up with the payments on his boat, was complaining that the demand for flatfish had fallen away by a percentage point or two. Did it mean people were losing their appetites?

Meanwhile in Birmingham, amid a minor rash of absenteeism, orders for new cars were sliding imperceptibly down the graph; a top-level salesman, with heavy debts on house and furniture, was retired to the suburbs where the pubs were uncannily empty. Were people travelling to fewer places? Between Itchen Abbas and Winchester two or three more rented sets than usual were returned to the television dealers – were people no longer viewing? – while the buffets on the trains north to Carlisle were soberly vacant of their normal gang of businessmen on expenses. Less drinking?

West of Petersfield a good restaurant abruptly went bankrupt; farmers on a tight margin in Wales cancelled newspapers while planning a demand for subsidy; a pastor in Kennington left home after an average domestic quarrel and vanished. Were people being pushed to the edge of their resources?

All coincidence?

Hardly. The book did not believe in coincidences.

And Dickinson, himself eating less, drinking

little, preferring to stay in one place to maintain the healthy stillness that had now invaded him, thought he had noticed, during those first hot months of the book's life, that the British people were becoming obliquely aware of it, if only as a phenomenon.

Or was this an illusion of that torrid summer, when reality, for those striking their own inner bargain with the book, rotted as fast as perishables in the markets?

Worse still, was this state of affairs perhaps no more than some self-aggrandizing fantasy of the author, whoever he was?

But now more serious cases began to spill out into the press. There was no doubt here: only the book could be the culprit. A political rally in Ventnor had broken up in disorder when Latimer Johns MP tried to address his constituents about the guts of the book. He had been shouted down. When a prep-school master read extracts to his class, the book had chased dozens of boys on a cross-country tide of excitement which the authorities took for rebellion. They had been punished. A minor canon in Chichester had tried in the pulpit to run away from the book's implications, but it had pursued him into the hills where he lay weeping on the cropped turf, miles from whatever imaginary hermitage he was seeking. He had been suspended. The book had howled so deafeningly in the ears of one of Birmingham's industrialists that after resigning from the board he was found under a full moon trying to drown himself in a dry ditch. He had been certified. Leaving the book face down on the beach, a Bembridge restaurateur had experienced its originality to the extent of swimming out into the Channel and not reaching France. He had been washed up. The book had gone straight to the heart of a Norfolk housewife engaged in average domestic quarrel to the point of smashing her husband's skull with a garden spade. She had been arrested. And the ravening wolf of the words had savaged an Army officer stationed near Leeds so effectively that he went berserk in the Mess. He had been found in pieces under a train.

On this initial showing Hugh Dickinson understood that elements in Britain as a whole could not stand the shock of the book. But what was the alternative? For too long the guts of the old country had been shouted down like the parliamentarian, beaten into the last ditch along with the schoolboys, living as suspended a life as the cleric; her lunacy as certifiable as the chairman of the board, her hopes washed up like the hotel manager, her development as arrested as the housewife: a country which along with the colonel had gone to pieces. Hadn't these events merely proved it high time for someone to come forward with bell, book or candle – it happened to be book – in an effort to better matters for the mass of the people in such a mess of a land?

As Dickinson well knew from his own reading, all the personal disasters reported impersonally by the press were echoes, perhaps projections, of his own heated experience that warm night when the book had kept him up to all hours.

His spine shivered.

What would happen to him or to anyone? All over England people like him – he shared their nerves, he felt the book troubling them – were so awake as to wish to avoid sleep while longing for the long dream which the book embodied, were no longer visiting restaurants because the prospect of grilled rump overhanging the plate amid piles of peas and a baked potato swelled them into debility, were skirting the pubs where the beer would swamp their brains and the whisky knife their livers, had stopped wanting to go anywhere in cars because the here and now seemed calm and sane, were refusing to watch visual lies on the box all evening or blink at them over breakfast in print, could no longer live with a marriage or a self that only just passed muster, and of course in the few extreme cases went nuts: drowned, gassed, died, killed, despaired, vanished. Evidently it had required only a few such people, reacting with catatonic zest to the book or the rumour of the book, to make the fabric of society appear to crack slightly.

And it was cracking.

A church in Chichester had emptied down to a few behatted crones too senile to read; that clergyman too had let the book overnight dissolve his few remaining crystals of faith. Pubs voided; those great glittering wombs of vacuity in the towns, strung like faulty punctuation along the life sentences of street after street, were equally losing their weekend trade. Formerly delicious restaurants in Soho noted a sinister absence of reservations; waiters flicked napkins at flies. Up and down the Avenue the theatre's make-believe fell into dramatic recession, no glazed queues drew up outside the cinemas in Leicester Square, the small hours grew ever smaller in the Mayfair nightclubs. All day and every night cities were dropping into sabbath sadness: dawn Billingsgate stinking with unsold fish, carcases decomposing frigidly along the reeking aisles of Smithfield, fruit and vegetables putrefying wholesale down the Borough. Newspapers pounding out of the latest and farthest reaches of Fleet Street fell on deaf ears; eyes were blind to the hilltop aerials webbing the

country with news, lies, tunes, ads. Enough people
to rock the economy, a tiny enough percentage of
Britain, had nicely decided to hole up and subsist
on little, to buy nothing, to wait and see, rather
than succumb again to the exaggerated needs and
pleasures that swotted days out, and left no time to
read.

Excitedly Dickinson recognized these as the
outward signs of his inner responses. Could it be
that everyone agreed with him at last?

Reading the book had persuaded him that none
of the dovetail answers fitted the angular questions
he had been mutely asking all his life. With him
they had been melted by the heat of the book into
flowing past the obvious daily solutions – boring
natural things like drink, fun, food, sex, talk –
while waiting, looking out of the corner of the eye,
for different ones, at the same time unsure of what
they might be, indeed wondering if they existed,
but prepared to take the risk.

Any risk. Provided of course that talk, sex,
food, fun, drinks, in the new context, made a disguised comeback. To let converts save face.

And then from the reports filtering into his office at the paper Hugh Dickinson noticed that with
an odd propriety *The Little Book* itself was being
rejected. On London streets, tossed aside like yesterday's newspaper, flicked by the wind, sodden or

sunned, copies of the work were being dropped by
unseen hands into the over-exposure of that summer, as if the text itself, too hot to handle, had en-
couraged the reader to ditch it as soon as he was
through. Outside a City church the gutters flapped
in a thunderous wind with broken-backed copies,
their pages strummed in the alley breeze between
theatres off the Strand where no queues waited,
they fluttered among the pigeons outside Soho
restaurants that had closed for lack of business. At
this rate the book would soon be ending up on a
bonfire.

Somehow, to Dickinson, these reported exam-
ples of the physical fate of the book provided, with
irony, the answer. Once read, the book demanded
that it be jettisoned for something better which the
book had itself posited; one's old life must be
risked, or nothing different could happen. It occurred to Dickinson with dread that this could
portend only one outcome: both the new book and
the old life must be regarded simply as garbage, as
by now not good enough, until with due solemnity
he had tossed them aside in favour of the idea of
still more to come.

More still to come.

A world beyond the book.

At the weekend, if he dared, he would read *The
Little Book* again, unless indeed his own copy were

lost, stolen by his wife as a passport to wherever her elysium, desecrated by the children who guessed by fatuous intuition how much their father valued it, dug into the ground by the gardener.

Or just mislaid.

Fallen off the edge of the known world. Or merely off the desk.

Tonight we attended in continuing good weather one of the smarter regatta parties in the back garden of a redbrick semi in Rope Walk that used once to be the manse of the chapel opposite. A Seaview brand of champagne from Australia was dispensed through the windows of a garden shed. A rickety table was loaded with dips and crackers. Around me surged the age group that made all the sense and running here, the thirty to forty-fives, spiced with a sprinkling of younger women imported for the weekend. Interspersed with cheeps of elation the mostly male chatter sounded as gruff as birdsong played slow, rising by the decibel as more people flocked in. I was of a seniority that ought to have been donating a cup for an annual event, not soaking on the sidelines without a role or only that of enjoying at a slight remove the tense summery sexuality of a party hedged in by suburbia. A remark I made slid unheard past a younger ear. Talk circumvented me.

Much of my youth was passed in houses like this. A long side passage, past lavatorial windows and a door to the kitchen, led into a garden as wide as the house but far longer. Now pounded by the shifts of conversing feet insensately heeling fag-ends into the grass, this lawn hid itself in shrubbery within a trellised and fenced patchwork of gardens to the secret rear of the High Street. To one side I gazed at a decrepit greenhouse in a tiny back patch dominated by a mossed old apple tree. On the other I looked at a spread of hibiscus in immense southern bloom, roses rioting around it. And fingering champagne from the antipodes I contemplated it all with awakening pleasure, as if I had never seen such things before in anything like the same light, this eerie light of evening. I thought of one day hiding out for an off season in this anthology of gardens that only for a few weeks in the summer were inhabited by other humans. A man alone could loll about for months in this enclosure at almost no cost, watching the fruit fall, tucked up by night in the unvisited greenhouse, making either nothing or no end of a thing of himself.

Pretending to relish isolation. Getting cold feet. Thinking out *The Little Book*.

At this late point in that hot summer we were sharing, my love, I realized that *The Little Book* meant what it said. It was letting me make it up as I went along, rather as in the old days before being ill I had let life make me up. Now I was casting my own images. Formulating my own patterns. Putting together a world which I could not only see whole for myself, but also – this seemed a daring line of thought – communicate to someone else, by looking at or thinking of that person, present or absent, in silence. That person being you.

So none of it had to be written down. Writing it down might reduce it. It required no statement. Stating it would only confine it.

After the halfway mark I thought I might have come resoundingly out of the book's clutches, feeling that in an adequate fashion I had liked things and people all my life – but never enough, or, no, not even not enough: rather that a ravening wolf of a definition of love had sprung from the tender depths of *The Little Book*. The old kind of love made us hate, be jealous, despise, feed on the soft silly fruit of ancient ego, brood on our wrongs, and kick out.

But this definition said: while timing my own pulse to the beat of nature, I tune in to whatever insistent beat lies beyond nature – even if that beat is only something I imagine, and would therefore like to exist.

It said: I am so at one with the privilege of liking being alive at my fullest extent that now at last I am free to love.

And all around me I embraced at last the possibility, if not the likelihood, of you and me and everyone else changing under my very nose from half-civilized animals into humans worth the word.

So far, we knew, very few people had read *The Little Book*. It did not matter. They sensed its presence. Thanks less to the media than to the currents generated by the climate that summer, inklings of the book had touched many individuals with an anticipation as pervasive as next year's holiday, a cool drink in the hand, Sunday morning in bed, peace, peace, a rise in salary, commonplaces, the birth of a child, a lilac spring, a night out on the town, hope, waking with the sun in your eyes, and the office never dull but almost.

A book to start lives.

Everywhere in the rear of the mind *The Little Book* thus waited to leap into being. It stole like an aroma into the atmosphere of the country. It raised people's spirits while their backs were turned. The remote idea of it woke them up to a shift in mood as the beginnings of autumn swept in from the west. Leaves fell in swirls round my head. Electric storms lit upon various areas as if to purge them. Contrary winds excited the dark forests of Wales and drove into the streets in Midland cities and cut clean through the Hampshire valleys. Rains came overland to sharpen the talk in lounges, slash on windows, warm the growing intensity between the sheets, dash against the stony indifference of houses as though to hammer their insides into sense. The excesses of the weather touched off freedom.

Weather for reading books. And for having champagne poured into your glass on a sunny evening.

I was still at the party. Youth thrilled in the backlots of Seaview. Nobody I could see was surreptitiously reading *The Little Book*. Nor would anyone read it, unless told to by fashion. Meanwhile the ethos assembled in that garden depended for the pleasure of the occasion on its rarity of occurrence, the snatched weekend, the wild freedom of an hour's sailing, the erotic rough and tumble of loud waves echoing into the quiet bedrooms. If they had peeped into *The Little Book* they would have been no better off than at this good party fading now into the dusk. But the future might count more, and soon would, when the word got around. In pleasurable confusion of mind I was thinking out the above just before the storm that hit the Island this weekend.

Without a hint at bedtime last night, when you lay securely reading, this secret weather began to blow some time during the small hours. We awoke to wind buffeting the windows with slants of rain audibly chilling us as we snuggled down in bed. During the morning it whistled up harder from the south until high tide at lunchtime was hurling broad breakers sideways along our strip of coast. They did not at first strike the eye as particularly hefty, but they approached with great frequency and speed, toppling over themselves far out, then dashing in on their own flourishes of spray to meet the outgoing suck of the tide in a crashing attack on the sea wall. Dollops of spray started bounding into our garden, drowning the summer out, drenching the wooden furniture at which we had lunched all month, hurling through the air many kinds of sea creature, curious wriggles of shrimp or flea, minute but jumpy. A primal excitement at this excess of life seized me in a wild grip as I stood outside getting wet.

Back inside we kept running for the binoculars. One moored vessel after another, including the Sea View Yacht Club nanny-boat, overturned and dragged on its anchor. Past our picture window small fragments of wreckage in gay summer tints were dashed on to our footpath amid the seaweed slopping up in swathes on the waves. Unseen in the background, in limbo, lay Portsmouth, the mainland a shadow, a solitary naval vessel at anchor amid angry mists beneath a sky that appeared to be hurrying northward faster even than the sea. The round offshore forts were ghostly reminders of invasion. Their just visible remoteness chilled the spine. News came that the catamaran ferry that connected with the London trains was cancelled, while the car ferry just about ploughed on. We were not cut off. But only by a whisker.

As for me, here I was, heavens, what luck, what weather! Out there it was danger and cruelty and force that I was looking at in that wilderness of raging greys, my little world, yesterday so bright, now encircled by these huge threats. I loved it, the heartlessness, the animation it aroused in me. The scene outside stood in thrilling contrast to the cosiness within – not only in the house, but in the feelings. The inner man coiled up in collusion with that imminence of disaster out to sea. I rose to the blind enmity. It rushed through me, that storm, and had the effect of both lengthening and clarifying not only the weekend but the lifetime behind it, which was now savouring its every extreme.

As for you, you casually told me I looked much better. Which had the force of a declaration of love.

Chapter Eight

In that storm I thought of my roots in Wales.

I was aware that the packer Owen William
Parry's view of the book was simpler than mine.
He took it as gospel that everything was wrong, except people. This saturnine version of my work-
ing-class self, dragging my feet, was now staring
bitterly at his own pinched flat in Lambeth. The
council had herded him into it. He felt undignified
putting up with such accommodation. He considered his wages, paid out of *The Little Book*'s
profits. He thought of the local men he knew,
many on welfare, receiving a lesser sum weekly to
keep up the needless appearances denounced by
the book.

The book made the common lot look common.
Dead common. And dead.

By now Parry had begun talking, in pubs, on
street corners; he had requested his branch library
to stock the book. He condemned the harsh scene
in which he and his neighbours, by bad politics
and worse education, had been tricked into living.

He saw vividly that nothing in society worked for the general benefit. Nor was the library service much use. Nobody could be sure of a copy without paying, stealing or waiting. 'They don't want us to know, you know,' said Parry.

If not for long, passers-by, old mates, computer operatives, machine minders, office staff, refuse collectors, all paused when he spoke. In the urban heat Parry became the angry focus of the book, crusading in the car park, revolutionizing the worn turf of the public gardens. These almost non-existent groups, as small as the book, dispersed with humour at the approach of a blue helmet, but night after night, in the dust of summer, in his spare time, Parry kept it up. His district was not just a bloody disgrace, he cried to anyone who would listen; it was a graveyard of the underdog. The cracked phrases rang out in the metallic air. Windows shot up to reveal bloated figures gaping, easing their sweaty collars, white or blue. Shouts rebounded off the long platitudinous walls of backstreet discos. 'It's this book, isn't it?' cried Parry.

Yet no hint of updated socialism snaked among the undercurrents of Parry's tirades. Here was fellow feeling instead. It was everyone who commanded his furious pity, everyone — foremen, priests, petty bosses, aristocrats, developers, ministers of the crown, lawyers, schoolmasters, hoteliers, industrialists, cancer patients, elderly ladies, the whole pack of them. They were merely human, dying on their feet while balancing their books, making money in order to have too little life left to spend it. 'Let's laugh them out of their joke,' Parry boomed.

Parry was proud of having no idea how positively to improve anyone's fate. The book had struck him as gentle enough to indicate room for improvement, but never so arrogant as to propose a solution. This did not perturb him. His formula was to call for volunteers, in the interests of whatever the cause might turn out to be. At first only school children gathered below his flat, waiting for this nutter to come home from packing books. Then the unsteady outflow of afternoon pubs joined the kids, then a few snappy housewives, then astride motorbikes some leathery lads who had run across a phrase and wanted more than what it said. A mood of truancy was in the air, a few men were knocking off work early. But all Parry did was send them away to picket for an hour this or that institution in the square mile of muddled industry, craft, commerce, religion, hospital and home, where they all lived, in his view, beyond the reach of the book. 'Keep these dregs

up to the mark,' Parry said with a cunning air but
without hope.

He was touched by them, having never bestowed
a thought on his fellow creatures. Their presence
kept him awake at night, just as the book had. Or
was he dreaming? All he told them in broad daylight was to be quiet and orderly – and by saying
nothing, not a word, render other people uneasy
with their own lives. But was this right? Might not
firearms be more persuasive?

In protest they gathered in small numbers at the
cathedral in Southwark. They picketed the high-
rise branch of a ministry in the bleak complex of
hard building which the developers had imposed
in their midst. They gazed at the police station.
Evangelists of silence, they stood outside public
bars. In the City they passed to and fro in front of
the offices of shipping lines, brokers, insurance
companies, as the lunchtime crowds hastened past
their banner and banality.

Yet Parry, when alone, was not at all sure that
any of this was really happening.

Was he imagining things at his age? Perhaps he
was drugged by the heatstroke of those dozing
pages that had somehow caught him offguard.
Perhaps *The Little Book* had turned his mind.

And then one hot night Parry was suddenly
aware in bed – was this a dream or not? – that a

national figure of weight called Latimer Johns MP, if asked, would address an open-air rally on his personal experience of this disconcerting book and how voters must react to it.

As far as he recollected, Parry had never heard of the man, who sounded posh. He had the force of a character in the book. And then at once Parry did remember him, traces of him, a statesman trying to change the country, but only in theory, only at candlelit suppers of the extreme elite, only in romances. Now, such was the confidence the book nourished in him, Parry had only to imagine that great meeting to know that it would take place: to see the underdogs by the dozen sweating on benches, bloated figures gaping at the truth, the effluvient of the pubs pouring down the gang-ways, kids banked in their hundreds against the stadium sky, as Latimer Johns MP rose on his makeshift platform, pockets bulging with a slim volume, and began to utter the very thoughts that lay inexpressibly in Parry's mind.

'I am here, ladies and gentlemen,' he said, 'to make my first political speech: to tell the truth. All I have said to you on earlier occasions has not been in itself untrue, but merely set within the limits of an untrue system. I do not represent you. I cannot. So I'm not seeking your vote, indeed I suggest that for a while you refrain from voting at all. Mass abstention is the only power. I'm also proposing that you now withdraw from all customary activity. Yes, leave your jobs. Be idle. Walk, fish, climb, swim, garden, doze – spend your time as if you were millionaires of it. You will see why. The brilliant source of what I'm telling you is here in my pocket.'

(Oh sure pull the other one etc.)

Johns inched out *The Little Book*, a tight squeeze. 'Not the Bible, my friends,' he said. 'That would no more fit into my pocket than into my life. Nor is it a keep-fit guide or do-it-yourself manual, though it's both. Nor a utopia, because it's not crammed with bad ideas clad in good words. Nor a manifesto, because it doesn't force you in dull language to whip up a belief in the incredible. Nor is it fiction, because it's one of the few facts of our time. It's *The Little Book*.'

(Oh ye gods fuck it he's gone too far this time round.)

'The book isn't trying to destroy society. Who wants to? Society isn't there. The moment this book entrusts you with the wide-open spaces of your imagination, our institutions turn into grubby facades intended to conceal the fact that we have no society. Look at this England: a hotchpotch of luxury cells, prisons which you think release you, torture chambers where you can't hear

your own screams, a country designed expressly
for the inconvenience and pain of human beings,
cruelly planned to vaunt the glories of a culture
that has run out of heart.'

(By crikey lord love us begorrah he's going to
have to do better than this.)

'O what self-destructive vulgarity encloses us,
my friends. I know. I was elected by you. Vulgar
persons like yourselves lack the capacity to call on
the best. They throw up their rubbish to govern
them. But who are the best? An elite, you say? No
– it turns out, since so many different sorts, and
classes if you like, now have the chance of reading
this simple book, that the best is no elite, no dan-
gerous caucus of philosophers, no gang of trigger-
happy intellectuals, no breakaway group of artists
squatting in a meadow of fantasy – but people, just
people, lifted at a stroke out of so-called society to
feel their way to a true one. Potentially the whole
nation, you and me, everybody.'

(Oh yeah?)

'So down your defences, and then read the book.
Change one or two of your habits overnight, and
then read the book. Don a pair of shorts, run brisk-
ly down Great Dover Street, eating your words
with one hand and humble pie with the other,
drinking it all in, finding what's left of fresh
country air almost choking you with its high-

octane integrity, until you end up inside-out at some beauty spot high on the downs overlooking the sea, where fewer thoughts and more feelings occur than anywhere since childhood, and then read the book. Or simply lock yourself in a bath-room and read it. Or go to bed, sleep tight, and wake up having read it. It doesn't matter where or how. This book is a fundamental silence which is going to last a very long time. You cannot fail it.'

(Balls why shouldn't I fail it if it's the last thing I do who wants your old culture any more I don't for a start.)

At that moment Parry woke up. Leaves rattled his window in a lurid dawn.

He had fallen asleep in his chair.

And again dropped the book.

And cricked his neck.

Thanks to all this mental activity I was feeling much stronger by the day everyone suggested tramping round the castle at Carisbrooke. An-other outing. A few solitaries were walking their dogs round the outer earthworks overlooking dis-tant troops of trees. Without today's haze I might have seen from the ramparts the whole of Wight. I could feel I owned the ramble of the Island's in-terior mystery, always touched at the far corner of the eye with hints of sea.

Against the invader the castle was defended
with thick surrounds of fortification, while within
stood just a hamlet, a chapel, a few residences, vacant spaces, its vegetable garden now a lawn. And
a hut in which either a donkey or prisoners drew
up the water from far below. I thought of how
many fools were shot from the superior holes in
the stonework, the usual lack of any serious (or
known) issue in the fighting. The weather hung a
gilded shroud over the centuries of dead lives
which had given their all for nothing. I trod these
heights as a tourist. The only quarry was not a
whole civilization invading from France but the
odd rabbit up the field.

In the more intimate museum, glimpses of the
castle's life preserved under glass, I found a pipe
organ. At first sight I mistook this organ for a
dressing-table from some mediaeval boudoir. But
there was no mirror. Instead of it, at face level, was
a frame of pipes, tiny flutes woodenly running up
and down the scale. I thrilled to it. A boyhood of
devotion to church organs came flooding back, a
sense of youth, then of power. A card announced
this elaborate item to be the oldest organ in
playing order from the early seventeenth century.
I longed to reach over the barrier, first with a foot
to pump air into the bellows, then with hands to
draw music, improvised music, music which only I

needed to hear, from the little keyboard of brown keys and black accidentals.

That would not be allowed by the authorities.

But the thought made me feel better. The sight of the organ surged into my recovery. I could hardly throw away my stick in triumph. I had left it in the car.

On impulse I thought of taking you, my love, to a City church I knew of old, where locked in narrow lanes behind the high-rise office blocks the organ had stood for a couple of centuries on the west gallery, and I had access to the key. For half an hour I improvised for you on no particular theme. I could not read other people's music properly and knew few of the rules. But I was able now and then to lose and unloose myself in realms of poorly executed extempore that trumpeted all my self-doubt into oblivion.

How do you do it? you might well ask.

Either all alone here in a businesslike church, I said, or in a pathetic country parish with one manual and a wheezy blower or in a cathedral with hundreds of stops to choose from and a huge nave to sound off in, for preference on a bright afternoon shut into the building or on a windy night in darkness except for that shaded lamp over the keyboards, I don't really mind when or where or how.

But what I do is empty my head, go blank, stop

thinking, and then into my fingers with any luck springs an idea that can't be put into words. An idea? In fact just one or two notes, these notes leading with a jump to four or five more, then I press a pedal with my foot more or less at random and a pattern's starting down there, and when my hands spread in natural flow across the keys with no sense of aim, a groundplan for a language of my own is swelling forth. So out of nothing a structure arises – it's like compressions of time and space – or also enlargements of both – which have the knack of sweeping me out of this church altogether, and my feelings, so far as I can feel them, race off down passages of memory, out into a future world far beyond this little platform perched up here in the gods.

I never know how long my nonsense has lasted, it drowns me in sounds I can't hear, it blinds me as if I were inside the dark guts of the instrument, it snatches my senses away, but equally there's another element I know I'm in, without having more than a notion what it is. Don't expect any logic or any revelation here, but inside me during the piece there's a sketch of a happiness that's beyond my power to communicate.

Oh, you said. You make it sound rather like *The Little Book*.

I liked extemporising on organs with my hands.

I liked improvising stories in my head. Both existed without a thought of writing anything down or a desire to make anything last. The fight was all. Ill as I was, no, recovering, but ill as I might later be, I felt here at Carisbrooke both the sag of the besieged, about to die if only of thirst but battling to whatever kind of end death dictated, and the belligerent thrust of the besieger, determined to get the better of an obstacle bigger than myself.

We came back in the sunlight to Seaview after a peculiarly satisfactory afternoon that positively looked forward to the evening.

Chapter Nine

❧

Tonight on the local news: a man serving life at Parkhurst escaped during the afternoon.

The children guffawed at his shaggy looks; I hadn't shaved today either, too unsteady on my pins to peer into a mirror. How far on foot, keeping to the hedges, between the prison and Seaview?

An offshore boat might be awaiting him. Or he might nick one of ours. Either the rowing boat turned turtle in the garden or the dinghy anchored well out but walkable at low tide. Murderers stopped at nothing – why should they? – when on the loose. We were less than ten miles from the prison; in other words, on a cross-country zigzag adrenalized by alcohol (they always found drink), too near.

The children went off to their bunkbeds. A nice room with that floor-to-ceiling window. I took my stick and wandered outside. Cascades of moonlight warmed by the scent of tobacco plants. No problem for anyone to lurk in the jet-black shadows of the alleyways. But how likely?

Inside the house they would be worrying where I was. Or they might not be.

What, if I were he, would I do next? And his name? From the mugshot, as in a shaving mirror, I could remember only his number, 587016: close to that of our telephone at home in London. A twinge of fellow feeling. Here was a man like me on the run from something.

In his case from lifelong retribution. And in mine?

The night air was chillier than it had first felt. A car purred slowly past, kerb-crawling – but had an aged driver. Disguise? At any second he would turn into our yard. I had a rubber-tipped stick to defend my family. A whiff of carbon monoxide wiped out the nicotiana. I moved indoors, locking and bolting up to imprison us all against this fantasy of an intruder invented by television. How long before they caught up with him on an island so small? I drank a whisky. Ate a banana. Felt my stomach turn over with desire, need, mostly fear.

The Little Book seemed also to be in danger of escaping.

Next morning one or two papers carried pictures of 587016's offence. At breakfast I was again mocked for my looks. The children pushed off in the unstolen boat. I read the report in full. On an inside page was a slim photo of the woman he had drugged, then at length raped more than once, in the end strangled but not before slicing up the three or four erogenous zones he had enjoyed by force, at last bearing her off to butcher coldly elsewhere, reducing the evidence in size while increasing it in quantity. I looked up from the page.

I saw the children out at sea. The wind was mild, the surface calm. Threats did not occupy these horizons, though the same local news last night had predicted storms. Cutting the victim in pieces had been the error. All the grisly locations, here a scarred torso, there a birthmarked limb, were at similar distances from the bungalow of the offender. Who had now elected to return to society within inches of my recovery. He must be ravenous after a night in the open. All day the lack of sightings reported on the news seemed to bring his presence closer.

That night waking up distracted. A knock on the door, or just a window rattling. A wind blowing up at sea. An invalid's heartbeat. Was any of it real, was I dying? No, no, someone close to the house, very close, perhaps inside. Sit up sharply in bed. Listen, ears thumping. The bed a coffin, sheets tight. Was he out there, down below, where? The whole moonlit island pounded through my head, seconds ticking. The gripe of hunger in my gut, dry mouth, bitten lips cracking, miles away a siren wailing on a false alarm. The map of the island shrinking towards this spot. The action closer than anyone knew. Was everyone safe?

Creeping downstairs, unsure of direction, fumbling. No one in the kitchen gorging out of the fridge. No one flat out on the children's beds, having stifled them for a kip. No one huddling shit-scared in the bog. The house by the sea singing silence only, worst of night sounds. Bend into the cooler, pull out white wine, swig from the bottle. Slap taramasalata on bread, champing, taking drips of oily roe on the chin. All at once forgetful, passing a hand over the brow – wondering where to sleep. Standing in someone's kitchen. Safe for a moment, having alerted nobody, everyone out for the count. Facing myself, my predicament. Have to flee, can't go back, won't ever go back, must win, now eating and drinking at last, so strength growing, but keep quiet, cool it, hold the violence down, looking out to sea through plate glass, to the lights of Pompey, ferries to the continent ablaze with glee crossing the quiet of the Solent, think of swimming over, only three miles, but the currents dragging at my life, and not a soul in the world I can ask to send help, send a boat.

But there was no sign of any intruder in the

house, so I stumbled with difficulty upstairs slowly back to bed.

In the early news he was still on the loose, I with him. Just when I had awoken in a sweat he was at Bembridge airfield. Two miles away, undetected, coming closer. Broke into a couple of light planes, one with a flat battery, the other too little fuel to get airborne. A near thing. Today tinder-dry sunshine seemed to burn the whole island out of hiding, except shadows – they were deep and dark and long. Drifted among the allotments poking marrows with my stick, suspicious of any movement within the wigwams of beanstalks, even a cabbage white jumping off startled amid scarlet buds. Thinking back to the airfield: skidding a few feet unevenly on the black turf, freedom soaring ahead of me – then a dead engine.

At dawn, hunched, sidling over the old golf-course at Bembridge, having waded the harbour at low tide past keels angled in mud. Nobody about. Stumbling up into that dry heath where girlish horses cropped and neighed. Nobody about. Knowing that Seaview awaited me, yet another chance of salvation, but in what form? Tired, famished, out of sorts, landlocked, by now too hopeless to guess what accident, a boat, a miracle, a gunshot to the head by armed police or my own hand, would catch me up, get me out of it, fix things for good.

The murderer had entered my mind. (Had he been there all along?) He swamped it.

He flushed *The Little Book* out of its delicate residence into nonentity. He made it homeless. He kicked it in. And because I couldn't locate him, except by nervous guesswork, I had no means of routing him out. (Had I been born with him in me?)

All I knew was he was continuously coming nearer: soon, behind that buddleia, crouched on that gutter, poised to leap, soon. (Would he turn out to have caused my cancer?) I could imagine nothing else, only this monster waiting to pounce on the holidays.

Anyway he had found my weakness.

I was frightened of him. And he knew it. And that knowledge had the power to query, mock and poison everything I thought or did.

He had to be caught, or I was lost.

The Little Book was at risk. Even now the people inhabiting its pages were running off in panic to the mainland. Last night Professor House's taxi had just made the last ferry in time. I was out of touch with the Fieldens who had crossed over in someone's yacht. Hugh Dickinson had abandoned me at the first hint of trouble. Not

only would I soon have no friends left, but as a result of these defections the book was falling apart
in my mind.

The very item that had been building me up
again, preparing me for a return to life, had been
invaded by a killer.

That day was the worst. That day showed how
fragile it all was, how vulnerable to infection, to
suggestion, how close to distintegration or death it
all lay minute by minute, how little you could take
for granted the body working, the mind remaining
on your side, the book coming out on time.

For that was the day *The Little Book* was suppressed. It said too little too obviously. It was out
of touch with facts. It had less authority than a
newspaper. Not only in heartlands of crime, from
Toxteth to Lambeth, had booksellers been strong-
armed into refusing to stock or order it; Harrods
too declined. The publisher's windows in the
Vauxhall Bridge Road were smashed by bricks
wrapped in obscene messages as the underworld
round the corner ganged up in defence of the missing convict. The printers at Chatham held off,
chary of running the presses, blaming a conven-
ient shortage of paper.

Another night raid on the Vauxhall Bridge
Road stole the disc and bashed up the back-ups. In

their ignorance the perpetrators tore into the word patterns in the author's original.

Which left sentences broken-backed.

Hanging by a syllable.

Phrases writhing on the floor in meaningless contortions, letters jumping out of a simple statement into the middle of the next orotundity.

All playing a devilish game with sense.

When staff came in next morning a senior editor found an epigram turned upside down on his slush-pile. A secretary noticed that traits of character had been clawed off one thumbnail sketch and attributed to an entirely different person. The enlarging world of *The Little Book* had abruptly shrunk. Inky entrails lay scattered on the office carpet.

The unknown author, brought in disguise as heavy as the security to inspect the damage, broke down, no, smiled a sad smile, sorry, try again, drained his hipflask with cynical indifference to the fate of his genius – no, apologies, it was at present impossible to say how he felt, for he too, damn the man, had quit the Island in the wake of all his creations.

There was nobody with me now. *The Little Book* had succumbed to the cunning and force of a murderer who let nothing, not a bloody thing, stand in the way of his survival.

I drank more than usual this morning. Shortly
after nine seemed a goodish time to drown my
breakfast, sherry the chosen killer. One drink se-
dated conscience, the next numbed reason, the
third provided the perfect excuse for drinking:
this pulling-apart of my newly half-constructed
world by a street savage, an uncontrolled force
from outside that corresponded only too well with
some inner mess of my own: yes, I wanted to see
The Little Book scrapped, shredded, tossed into
the air in a flurry of scorn and rage. Without the
guts to do it myself, longing to do it, I had allowed
in yet another invention, no, aspect of myself, no,
sorry, killer, to do my dirty work for me. And now
he had done it, without entering in person this
quiet house in Bluett Avenue and literally slaught-
ering my family, I felt an abounding relief that
The Little Book, with all its inaccuracies, improb-
abilities, lack of actualities, futilities and little-
nesses, was no more. I owed my freedom from it to
the man who had escaped.

This was inner bluster. All I did after lunch was
doze off.

I woke up from the doze. And called out. No
reply from anywhere, sun blinding into the room.
When I nodded off, the boy had been watching a
slow over being bowled on television. Screen now
blank. The whole waste of sea outside sparkling.

My girl was supposed to be downstairs reading. No sign or sound of her. An empty house. I saw that I could escape. Leave them. Creep off. The police were nowhere to be seen. No one would report me. Long ago I killed someone, but who? Forgotten. Probably only myself, my chances, a young man who had his future ahead of him, any number of possibilities. Felt no guilt. Now, nobody watching, I could get off the Island. Make my way back, but to where? And they would find me out. Here where I sat befuddled was the operations room. Appeals for help would get to the mainland before me. Messages would leapfrog the catamaran so that police in clothes plainer than mine sidled up to me at the quay and brought me back in hand-cuffs to the prison of the family, the punishment of being sick and old, the incarceration of the in-evitable.

I went and put my head under the tap and poured cold water on it and my son popped up from nowhere and asked what on earth I was doing and a minute later my daughter drifted in book in hand and showed a healthy lack of interest in whatever plight I had imagined for myself. The cricket got turned on again. Her eyes engulfed the big book she was living through. And next you came in from somewhere and asked how I was. You said I was frowning, and yes, why not, I felt I had lost something. A thought had gone missing. A feeling was astray, some part of me had escaped. The sea sparkled still. A hovercraft boomed across it to Southsea. The fast bowler's over drew slowly to a close. Back to the studio. Local news. Lead story: the prisoner who three days ago escaped from Parkhurst had been sighted. At any minute an update was expected. Meanwhile . . .

I felt disappointed. I had missed him. Missed meeting him. Not known, truly, what it was like to be a murderer on the run. Having for a second believed that was what I was. A lifer, offered at the last minute a few instants of parole. I had lost the chance – by not being assaulted by him or cheated of food or broken into – of recognizing my own delinquency, of admitting, expressing, enjoying it. I felt bereft. My freedom had been snatched away. I was back in jail with myself. Not roaming the Island end to end, fearing for my life. Not unshaven, desperate, venemous, alive. Not pitting my wits against the witlessness of authority. Not questioning everyone every step of the way.

And then at six o'clock came the details. At lunchtime – not that he had lunched (though I had, off crab and Adgestone) – the murderer had been caught. He had been trying to hijack a boat. (Not one of ours.) He was floundering among the Medina yachts looking paranoid. (He was drunk.)

Dozens of police closed in with caution on this un-armed yachtsman who had not made it to the mainland, whose hand was on the tiller of a vessel embedded in the mud of a tidal river. He put up no fight. Handcuffs, bit of rough handling behind slammed doors to pay for wasting police time, then back to square one plus a few years added to life. A doddle for destroying a little book. I felt the bite of the cuffs round my mind, began wondering how to escape, what would mean freedom to me, given that obviously *The Little Book* was no more.

Dearest, I need your help now. Don't know how to ask for it. Or in what language. Having lost my mind to that little book, what's to go in its place?

And how do I ask you such a question, you not even knowing what I was thinking, dreaming, re-covering? I should have told you earlier.

After the news that he had been recaptured, you were thoughtful. As if picturing, reflecting on my emptiness, wondering why.

Why?

The Little Book has broken up, that's why. It's in pieces. Gone. I don't know where to look for it. That fucker has fucked it. I wish he was still at large. I'd go out and kill him, the violence in me never burnt hotter, in fact I never noticed such rage before. Now I want to strangle cats, push the snouts of all barking dogs into the rock-pool, hold them under till they wriggle and die. All this civilized shit of a book going on in my mind, well now it's sicked up all over, a mess of sad, infected, pus-ridden ideas I thought were doing me good, getting me perked up for life again.

I am not getting better. Not on the point of getting better, I am worse, I have given up. It all looked, or seemed to look, and appeared to feel, very gradual, the improvement, there was the tiredness I welcomed (wasn't it curative?) and felt impatient about, then one day wanting to do more for myself while lapped by luxury provided by others, so pleased not to have to make efforts: just sit back, lie back, drink, eat what given, let imagination pretend it ruled the world, oh bloody Christ, old dear, retch up that crap fast, boyo, or you're dead.

Pasta this evening? Fine. With the Macon rouge, yes? I gazed out at the sea he never managed to cross. Rome, France . . . all gone. But a collusive supper to come, children safe in the bunkbeds. I felt vacant. Part of me was in prison, if not all. How to make a comeback, a clean breast of it, a full recovery? For the moment the murderer had silenced me. Slightly ahead of autumn, all England was scattered with the torn shreds of *The Little Book* floating to earth.

For yet another outing, to clear the muggy air, we drove to Havenstreet, along the depression of the village's main thoroughfare, downhill all the way, past a genteel barracks of an old people's home, at least with a pub opposite, to the Southern Railway station of the steam service from Wootton to Smallbrook. From the parking area last cars were departing into the sunset; we had come too late for the ride. Outside the likes of a station-master's cottage an elderly handyman with a glossy stoker's cap was chopping wood, perhaps to fire boilers. A figure in oily blue overalls ambled timelessly to his polished old banger. A notice at the booking kiosk, closed, said the first train on the line was the 10.05 tomorrow.

Now the whole toytown was at rest, little different in mood from a graveyard. Entombed here was a service our world no longer had any need for, except as an indulgence in its past – a past of which the mechanics still worked, in which the drama of travel portentously lingered in the puff and clang, the sheer visible power of steam. This evening it looked as set as a photo. The rolling stock mute on the sidings. The dogged engines (one called Freshwater) in line. The buffet shut. The eloquent signs (Ladies and Gentlemen) as leaf-green as memory. In the windows of the shop were the timetables to Bournemouth of my youth. Within their exactitude lurked assignations. They printed the promise of a romance never wholly delivered. On this spot the Southern Railway, network of my nonage, had concentrated its remains.

I knew the last thing I must do was catch the 10.05 in the morning. 587016 was back inside, so the present was now safe and I had better get on with it. The past looked safe too, immured in this chugging open-air museum of travel towards no destination. I could not, dared not, see myself pottering a short way down the reconstituted line to a terminus even more boring than where I stood, only to shunt back with even more illusions than when I left. I must have no more to do with it, love it though I should, lured though I might be. Here the past stood, bathed in evening light, as glowingly ancient as a childhood postcard from a father away at the wars. That was sedation. That was killing time. That was death.

In that instant *The Little Book* sprang back to life.

That night Hugh Dickinson at home in Hampshire received a call at all costs to return, if necessary by the last ferry. In Seaview, to my relief, I glimpsed Professor House's unmistakable silhouette hurrying into the Yacht Club to dine, even though he was dead. Rumours reached me of Sir Davis and Lady Fielden making a more leisurely progress, hampered as usual by too much baggage, back to their thatched lair somewhere on the Island. It felt to me, lounging on the sea wall watching in the dusk the links with the mainland pass one another a mile out and hearing the boom of the late hovercraft fill the sky, that everyone was coming home.

You were in bed reading, the children asleep, the murderer was behind bars. *The Little Book* had almost lost itself. But now they were on their way back. They felt safe here, my gang of not quite existing heroes and more than diaphanous heroines, because they no longer had to try. They were content to leave their fates in my hands. I was no killer. I wanted the best for them, and they knew it.

They were in for a surprise. Leaning over the wall in the wan ebb of the moonlight, listening to the faraway tide coming in, everyone asleep behind me, I knew at once that *The Little Book* had other plans for them. Over that slaughter I could and would have not an iota of control, poor them, poor me. I raised the last sip of a final glass to the night's ultimate P&O ferry on its inexorable path to France, packed with punters who read only duty-free price-lists, and went indoors avidly to await the dawn.

Get up before anyone else, lad, steal a march . . .

Chapter Ten

❦

One more magnificent weekend, the summer desiccating the country. At Seaview the children and I were staring into rock pools, narcissistic shallows where nerves of fish whizzed. A crab thrust up slow sand while digging in. A pool was the whole sea in miniature. Scallop shells in the shallow quiet, old oysters, and then, treacherously, the squelch of the blue slipper that squeezed suddenly up between the toes when rockpooling: an Isle of Wight villain of landslide that lurks under sand.

Hugh Dickinson, his pages on the paper put to bed, caught the train home. *The Little Book* was in his mind. He had to write a definitive account of it for next week, with no idea how.

He strolled for a while about the house, rooms blurred into plummy shadow by the glare of the sun outdoors. All was in place; yet nothing was. It occurred to him with a thrill that he had not come home at all, but strayed into a domain now belonging to no one.

A Porsche came up past the church and under the chestnuts and stopped.

Who was this intruder?

Thinking of his piece, trying to feel it grow, he found his wife in a hayloft over the barn. Or was it his wife? She was unlike her old overfamiliar self. Borrowing the children's colours – they were away at school – she was painting a picture of her face reflected in a handbag mirror. The pathos of art struck him: a species of make-up, to cover the horror of not recognizing your own person.

By now even I wasn't sure who it was.

Davina? The brush in her hand touched in an eyelash. She did not seem real. It was as though he had always imagined her.

Yes, this woman was also, or only, the divine Davina? That Porsche was otherwise hard to explain.

To give himself time Dickinson asked, 'What are you doing?'

'Reading the book,' she said. 'And painting. I can't paint. On the other hand of course I can because here I am, I'm painting. For once I'm looking at myself not as others see me, but as I do. I've taken a cottage by the sea. Does that sound romantic? Far from it. I'm going to clean it out. I'll drag it all into the fresh air and throw away what I don't want, and then rub down the walls and let the salty winds blow in through every door and window, and get rid of the cobwebs and accumulations of dust in every corner I'd forgotten was there. It's the only thing I've got of my own, so I'll start looking after it properly instead of letting it go to pot. And for once I'm not complaining – what I really do not need is anyone else to help me.

'This is the choice I've made and it's total,' she said. 'I want those sands on the edge, and one small true place in the picture I'm trying to paint – this cottage that came to me pat when I put down the book – and all that air.'

'Air?'

'At last I'm breathing,' she said, 'and that's just the start. I want to see myself, not only in a mirror, not only in the pages of a book, certainly not in you, not in the shared life you've been leading on our behalf, no, in no way but what my hands and heart make of something I can't manage – the medium, these paints, this brush – in relation to the complex me which this simple little book foretold. I may fail. But I would rather have failure on my terms than success on anyone else's. That defines breathing.'

All was clear to Hugh except the square of portrait, incomplete, childish. He had a fleeting sense that the picture she was really painting, in words or on canvas, was of him: a projection; her only

150

way, after such paralysed living with someone else, of getting close to herself.

'I don't know how you responded to the book,' she said. 'Isn't it always different? It hurts so to be oneself. But somehow it makes other people rush closer. Have you noticed that you don't have to talk to anyone to explain anything? I'd have said all this better if I'd kept quiet. But of course the wretched book may be just a fashion that'll be out by the end of the summer — the whole country can't just go to pieces, can it, just to stay alive?'

Dickinson liked this contentious note. Even Davina (or was it his wife?) seemed on the brink of detecting a flaw in the otherwise matchless unfolding of the story. Refreshed by doubt, he suddenly knew what he would say in his piece for the newspaper.

It would be a darn sight better than *The Little Book*.

For no reason next morning I woke up cross. The early light across the foot of the bed looked out of sorts. I tightened the dressing-gown cord round my scar and drifted pettily down to breakfast, hoping for some excuse to complain. This anger that grumbled as irrationally as a sexual affront needed appeasing. At least someone had been out to fetch the paper. I snatched it up, lounged in a chair at the head of the table, was asked what I would like for breakfast, felt faintly mollified, and on an inner page found this piece by Hugh Dickinson.

'The author of this book,' he began, 'has pulled off a remarkable feat.

'He has written a brief volume that is not only specific in criticism of contemporary manners, but also refuses to provoke controversy. The reader, of whatever class, colour or creed, cannot but agree with every point because he is granted the magic sense that he is personally creating every point for himself.'

(Coffee.)

'The truth within the reader is what concerns these chapters, and our amiable author has so framed his book as to accommodate the individuality of each and every one of us, by leaving his pages as suggestively blank as prehistory yet somehow as full as a literature.'

(Something funny about this coffee.)

'Culture as we know it, that sedative jade, this writer makes us write off in less than a phrase,' wrote Dickinson. 'That dismissed, he passes to a host of other matters that preoccupy and thus ruin our lives: marriage, politics, sex, dreams, wars, jobs, to name only a few. By failing to come into the open and softly describe his own marriage, he makes us reflect hard upon our own. By pausing on the doorstep of politics with such devastatingly curt analysis, he makes us realize how little we have missed by not taking politics seriously.'

(Bacon too stringy, getting stuck in the teeth.)

'Yet, with a brilliance hitherto unexampled in expository writing, we are *told* precisely nothing.'

(Yolk too runny, otherwise okay, nice tomatoes.)

'We are paid the compliment of having to project on to the page for ourselves the society we inhabit and to provide a remedy that suits the individual reader, even as it creates, out of his inner resources, a society loose and vital enough to contain, nay, liberate us all.

'No reader will leave this book feeling disappointed. Concussed perhaps; for it is indeed his own naked experience into which the pages rush him headlong. In the course of the action several characters, finely sketched in the margins, argue over their differing remembrances of the book's narrative, heart, message. Each tops the others in suggesting there is more to a particular passage – paragraph, sentence, even comma – than any has the capacity yet to perceive. These affable confrontations enlarge everyone concerned.'

(Burnt toast.)

'To strike a personal note, I am convinced that

the book's precepts are right. But can I follow
them?'

(Doubt it.)

'All right, I've managed to suppress my training, I've been pushing pins into my balloon of an
ego, I've created the book myself – all that's fine.

'But what next?'

(Nothing. Not for you anyway.)

'All those alarming notions about wavelengths
lying in wait for me, underswells of the spirit about
to break surface – well, they exist all right. It was
my idea anyway; I put them into the book, the way
the book asked me to. But now I'm too scared to
handle it, this dragnet under dreams, trawling illogic out of the deeper waters. I'm revolted by the
idea of changing almost more than I actually want
to revolt or change.'

(Marmalade.)

'Yet I also want my book to crack the barriers I
know exist,' Dickinson went on. 'It's up to me, to
the loose thinker, to the man in the street who is
just bravely turning a corner, who yesterday
dropped his watch down a drain, who in Carlisle
while thinking of Marseilles believes that he really
is in France, it's up to me to smash the remaining
barriers that divide me from myself.'

(More butter.)

'And it's so close,' claimed the article. 'It's as

close as tomorrow's Sunday dinner in Birmingham provided I don't go to sleep after it, as clean as a swim off the South Coast as long as I don't drown, as eruptive as a domestic quarrel that doesn't end in our killing each other, as fast and smooth as that Inter-City to the North if all the signals work, as calm as digging a Suffolk garden assuming I go deep enough, and much more totally satisfying than making slow love in any or all of these places.

'Breaking the barrier is what the fuck narrowly misses, what swings over the points just in time, what turns up trove out of the familiar soil, what digests the Midland dinner into renewed energy, what turns the swim into a split-second dream of the whole of life, and what converts the quarrel into a sudden understanding that will last. Yet I sit here at a desk day after day, and I try to break that barrier. It's there to be broken and is breakable. If I could break it I would have my fingertips on several of our tomorrows, that's all.'

(Not much of an article. More coffee.)

After seeing his piece in print that weekend Hugh Dickinson had the sense that he had let *The Little Book* down. Been unfair to the work by saying too little. Dishonest to himself by writing at all. All that week at the office he felt his guilt deepen. He was not congratulated on his piece; nor did anyone raise any objection. He had been elevated by *The Little Book* only to be cast down by it; on its terms his paperchase of articles constituted an insult to life's simplicity, trajectory and span, wilderness, amiability, aptitude for the wrong answer, passion.

In bed alone that night his mind switched to the woman who had started the process that brought him to this pass: that day she biked him the book. He hardly remembered her name, let alone her number at home. Anyway it was too late to call, politely to demand her body as a punishment for putting him out of joint. His recollection of that drunken afternoon stirred, the thought of revenge swelled. He wanted her at his mercy. His hand moved down and loosened the cord of his pyjamas.

Hugh stroked himself with care. The thought of her ill-tempered submission to his desire aroused him to a pitch of self-love that drew him beyond the straight good sex he and his errant wife had shared for years. She grew in his imagination. She taunted him. She sneered at his lust only to exacerbate it. She was winning, but what battle? With every second she came closer, closed in on him, bore down, until breathing harder he felt stifled by the heat of her presence.

At that moment, with a twist of apprehension that shook him, Hugh felt in danger of becoming

her. He felt her rage at being insulted by his lechery. He felt her drawing up his legs the silk of
her stockings, cross-dressing him, the hands of
someone completely at his disposal but totally her
own person caressing into pain the more erogenous points of his body, the twist of her fingers on
his tightening scrotum: lying beneath her tight
hips, acceding to the pressures of her own gender
shift, his body succumbing to intense attack –
then crying out unheard in the dark as the convul-
sion spilt into the sheets.

Not bad, Hugh whispered, fighting for breath.
She receded. The dark swam over him. He saw that
he had failed to punish her, this idol of fantasy
who had stripped, mocked, denied him. He had
come nowhere near getting his own back for *The
Little Book*.

Call her Davina – wasn't that her name?

Or was she an invention, a slant of his nature,
just a curvaceous scrap of himself which he had
better recognise, were he not to fail the book yet a
third time? All that night Hugh Dickinson
brooded on Davina. What did he do wrong? He
should have asked her for more, more informa-
tion, a glimpse at least of the secret she had kept
from him all along. Now she had gone, leaving
with him his perverse view of himself as a sadistic
wanton, taking away any chance he ever had of re-

reading *The Little Book* in a new light. She had come, and gone. To ease his pain Hugh thought this fatuously funny.

On the Island I awoke to sea and sky that morning, refreshed. The dream had left me feeling complete. I could, and did, lie in bed gazing with satisfaction at my creation of a woman. I had brought her into being. And kept her to myself. And held her.

As I held you.

Chapter Eleven

Dave Higgs awoke next morning to find *The Little Book* lying in smug black reproach on the sheets He squirmed out of bed on the other side. Having last night snatched it back from the jaws of fate in the oyster bar, he determined to get to grips with it today.

Within an hour, shaved for the first time in days, layers of sweat and grime showered off, juiced and egged and toasted, he opened the book and stared in disbelief at the shameless depths of its pretensions. It was telling him what to do, how to behave, who to be. By God, it was patronizing him, patting him on the head, the balding head, for having the nerve, the effrontery to exist.

The book was a fucking hangover, today's bitter revenge on last night.

Dave's day was as yet unplanned. To spare himself the bother of deciding how to wreck it, he had vaguely looked to the book. A few pages, and words had spectacularly failed. With a snort he stuffed his copy in an inside pocket and set off towards town in a fair old rage.

I will kill it, he muttered, ambling past Victoria Station.

Okay, if it gets in my way, I fight it, and I win.

Nobody talks to me like that.

He passed a couple of pubs that looked only half open. Dragging the book out, he consulted it at a random page as though taking his bearings from a map. He at once detected the book in a thumping lie or rather an insult: it said he was drunk, and he had touched not a drop. Had a pack of guardsmen not been marching past to the platitudes of a band, he would have tossed the book at Buckingham Palace.

I shall murder it in private when no one is looking.

I will strangle with my own hands this bugger of a book.

Walking adrift up the Mall, Higgs thought better of confrontation. He fingered the book, eased it slyly open, peered into its shadows at an angle; pages slanted against his eye, words shrunk foreshortened then vastly expanded. For a second in that metropolitan sun it seemed a book intended to cause blindness. Again rage clasped his vitals. He emerged into Trafalgar Square blinking, gripping this black book as if it were a grenade with pin removed.

Legs aching, carrying his intolerable burden, longing to hurl the text into the National Gallery, he dragged to Soho, his principality, the poisons of *The Little Book* sizzling within him. They were swilling around like the daily doses of beer, souring with the half-pint of whisky curdling in his gut, topping him up in wines of many colours, drowning him in the amnesiac aftermath of brandy: here was a hard-backed lunch-and-a-half that by some paradox was preventing him from entering pub, club or bar. It had compelled him to stay out on the street. Damn the book, he growled, damn, what am I doing wandering sober through Soho advertising to the masses a vicious curtailment of their pleasures?

Better declare war on this stupid effort to stop us destroying ourselves.

Drawn to his haunts, Higgs drifted up Rupert Street displaying his copy of the book to stallholders hemmed in by fruit. Witnesses saw a well-liked denizen of the area's alcoholic tendency brandishing the likes of a bible at their attempts at honest trade. He looked like a busker, yet desolate, as though ineptly handling inner crisis. As he crossed Brewer Street into the alley dividing the sex-show from the bakery he was seen to gaze almost in tears at the book. It was drying him out. It was ruffling him up. It was desexing him. In every way he was being bullied by its superiority of tone into maiming his life.

Cheap tomatoes, peaches on offer, gave no comfort. He was beyond assuagement. Why not then boot a parabola of cut-price raspberries in arabesques that splodged to the pavement, why the hell not kick cabbages into an unseen goal? Cries of outrage broke out. Ugly costers closed in on him over tarmac slippery with squashed bananas, leaping to wrest the book from him, aiming below the belt. But dancing backwards in mockery he kept the volume aloft on a long arm. He threw at his attackers words he thought nastier, better chosen, than those waving above his head, he challenged the dogs to jump up at him, snatch the ultimate treasure in their jaws, paw him to the ground, tread him into the squelch of their putrefying stock.

At the echo of dissension in the street men poured out of the bars to support whichever side took their fancy. Yet intoxicated by the fury he had provoked, playing to the drunks tumbling on to the scene, by leaping on to stalls that cracked and shuddered beneath his weight, by keeping the filthy book out of everybody's reach, Higgs managed to preserve the truth from the grubby scrabble of all these shits who thought him a drunk. Swaying high above the market, his audience jostling for his blood, he got the book open for a couple of seconds, gabbled out a sentence, shouted a slogan from low down on an early page, thus proving to this anarchic herd of assassins who had appeared from nowhere that the guff he had in his hand was not for them. A hand from below caught his leg in the grip of a mantrap.

'Hold it, boys,' Higgs cried.

Within seconds, in full view, he had broken the back of the book and was tearing out pages by the handful, ripping them in half, scattering them into the fruity air, leafing them down on to the tilted boxes of salad, until the spaces of Berwick Street were floating in a bookish autumn, as genius torn to bits came to earth. Hours later, Dave by then blotto in a club to which he had contrived to run only by virtue of being sober, traces of book lingered on. In the street a torn revelation blew into the doorway of a café just closing. A secret of life lay flattened in the gutter.

Later that evening he passed out. He passed out of my story. I had got rid of the sot. There were other parts of me too who must go.

Today, by now thought well enough to drive a car alone, I braked at a gate of a house I had cared for in the past. This time it was Victorian, a century later than our visit to Appuldurcombe at the start of my convalescence.

Shielded from the Ryde road by massed shrubs, the property down the curve of potholed drive seemed half derelict. The lawns were more or less shorn, the tennis court kept up, steps to the Japanese garden unweeded. Glimpses of the interior offered broad hints of a business gone bust, piles of paper slid to the floor, filing cabinets opened as if rifled. Suave red creeper fingered the brick outside. Shags of old man's beard were taking over the fabric, meticulously dated on various keystones from 1871 to 1898, years that climaxed the Empire. This heroic pretty place was designed and built and inhabited, his sweep of view overlooking Spithead from an eminence, by a general at the court of Queen Victoria. Here was his home.

Twenty years ago this house was converted into a self-catering hotel. It was very Isle of Wight, a dotty amalgam of square towers, conical steeples, windows a mass of mullions interspersed with stained glass. It had struck me then as happiness domesticized. I had my round room. I had my view narrowing over meadow between banks of trees to the Solent. I had my work, a book that would alter the world. Except now and then at the bar or billiard table, I kept away from slackers occupied more or less like me on some idle project. Here was a scrap of autumn holiday that required you only to fry your own breakfast.

Today these remnants of yesteryear were bathed in a delicious light that looked terminal. Three cows and a calf grazed in the composed manner of a period painting on the fields sloping to the sea. The stone urns on the terrace were blurred by mosses at intervals along a wall itself overgreened with entanglements of weed. The whole scene looked as though it had been ditched for good by the nineteenth century. Nature was rampant, civilization in retreat.

Tripping over the pitfalls of the outer paving I peered inside. The shelves had been emptied of books. They had been military, piscatorial, explorative, bad, for a century only an ornament. In the billiard room the table's baize was purpled and yellowed by spills of light from the stained glass. Warped cues stood against the wall. Old scores were marked. To an outsider it all looked faintly ridiculous, a house sunk in history as deeply as the *Titanic* in water; to me it also looked authoritative. Even as I strolled round it, peeping in, I felt better. The muscles in my calves tautened. The pump of adrenalin clenched my fists. I was alone with the house miles down on the sea-bed of time. It needed rescue, to come into its own again. Not just an eccentric amalgam of scraps of building, this house, but a real piece of past, about to integrate with an equally real present. That was what I asked of myself.

In a glance over these recuperative weeks, I felt the strength of my attachment to the house. Any excuse for a visit would do; showing it to a friend as if I owned it, indeed showing it off as though it were an aspect of myself that was dying or needed resuscitation. Now that it was available, on the market at least – only last year had it failed as a self-catering hotel – I could consider it my own. I could wander about the grounds without attract-ing attention. I could be an emotional squatter: I had rights.

I drove back to the oysters we were having for lunch. Contrary to well-meant advice I saw oysters as a way of ingesting health, taking in sea breezes, being suddenly beyond the shore. All the elements were basic and pure – pepper, lemon, bread and butter, even a sharpener of shallot and vinegar – and all blended, however opposed they seemed; even wine to drink with them somehow did mingle, despite apparent clashes. From the shaky start of my recovery I had clung to fish and white wine as to essentials. They seemed the savour of sea and sun. It was island fare. I was eating what the invisible surrounded me with, the underworld twinkling between toes when I paddled, the mystery gazing back at me from rockpools. There was everything unseen here, and I consumed it. As always the best oyster was the fat one whose skirts cringed at the squeeze of lemon, black lace edging towards its wet centre in a visible shrink of pain, peppered with a twist, its sweetness cut by the vinegar that pre-echoed the wine that within seconds sloshed down after it, blotted at the last aftertaste with bread torn off the slice.

I gazed vacantly out to sea, well-being at the thick of things.

Hugh Dickinson went home to Hampshire that weekend to find his wife absent and no Davina, the house stupid in the sun. He tried among the offhand silences to concentrate his mind on matters he knew to be important. But could not. His brains stewed in heat. He was dogged by remorse. He had lost respect for his mind. It was as if he had recently come within an inch of touching his own emotions; and missed them – after his too literal article in the thin columns of the newspaper had broken upon the world and, by praising *The Little Book*, somehow closed down the subject for ever. Wrapped it in newsprint. Consigned it to the gutter.

But that hot afternoon, in her larger home miles

away in a landscape more dramatic than his, Lady Fielden must have picked up a clue to his predicament in her memory of the book.

From nowhere, or from an image in those pages, came into Lady Fielden's mind the notion of drowning her past. She was shocked. She wondered how evidently right could be an act so apparently wrong.

Into Hugh's mind, in the same instant, swam the idea of acting at all costs upon the dictates of the book, however crudely. He thought of the huge bonfires – had the book been specific on this count? – that celebrated triumphs or heralded any human event of note or flamed messages across the dark distances of centuries past. With fireworks in mind he began moving furniture into the garden, piling chairs under the horse chestnuts, inlaid tables, cushions and heaps of paper, paintings and footstools, creating a pyre of a study, an inflammable boudoir – just as Lady Fielden was looking back at her ancestral home from the parched lawns and wondering briefly, drat that book, why she was flushed by such an exorbitant desire to say goodbye to it all for ever.

The message seemed to have arrived in code from a distance, a distance that had been inside her unrealized since she was a girl.

She knew she had powers. She had no wish to

define them. They were no business of anyone else's. She had no need to show off. She wanted only to help behind the scenes when she strongly felt for someone, but without their knowing. Like charity.

She knew she must release certain forces. She felt them to be helplessly imprisoned by the well-proportioned saloons, the attitudes beyond question, that had blighted her existence in that house. She had no idea how to persuade Sir Davis that she was right other than by ignoring him. But her husband had been elsewhere for years. At this moment she could almost see him perspiring in the gunroom over the flesh of the maidservant.

With a pang of decision chilling her body Lady Fielden stared at the house, dreading the release of her power to hurt and help people, tears breaking on to dry cheeks.

The rain fell in torrents that night. It seeped deep into the earth. Higher winds blew in from the sea, winds the Island had not experienced for half a century. Waves yards high breached the sea wall and crept into the foundations of houses built in Victoria's heyday. Tennis courts swamped from above began to crack from beneath, their strict white lines twisted to suggest a different ball game, while the tarmac in Bluett Avenue spouted gouts from hydrants breached by the upward force of water. The streets were awash. Seaview, built on hopeful but insecure foundations, was in serious danger of being swept into the sea.

An inch fell in an hour, then several more centimetres in twenty minutes. The skies had rarely opened so wide over a coastline prone to slips, slides, changes, shifts, no part more prone than this limited area where the blue slipper, that venomous mud as unstable as quicksand, lay in wait for just such undermining conditions as these, sea rain drawn in violence to the magnet of the rapidly incoming tide. Inland the clouds struck the hills and enveloped them. The rain soaked into the chalk, cracked it, crumbled it, edged the geology out of true, so that water gathered, swelled its forces at dark levels where in secret the new lie of the land was to be decided. Dirty rain squeezed over rock underlying the blue slipper. A stratum formed multimillennia ago abruptly gave. A slight give was all that was needed in the soft levels that upheld these seashore fields on the now threatened summit of which stood the old house with late Victorian additions where the infant Lady Fielden had first learnt to assume that island weather was continuously benign.

And then, slowly, a tile slid off a turret, splashing down into the torrent of chalky water sloshing past the billiard room, the weathervane came plunging in a whirl of disorientation into the flood, soaked walls vertically jackknifed on to lawns, leaving no support for the tons of Victorian masonry above, and, in silence, apart from the everlasting hiss of the rain, the whole elegant caboodle, at a relaxed speed, slithered in gathering ruins, now and then with a crack and a splosh, down towards the sea from which this land had first arisen.

Lady Fielden watched from afar. Someone else is doing this, she thought, somewhere else, not I, someone bigger, outside myself, a great presence, up there in the sky, deep in the earth, not me, not me, a hidden voice, a force beyond me.

Simultaneously Hugh Dickinson felt he had worked out the logic of his conduct. The arguments pro and con trailed far behind. Neither counted. As he sweated heaving the furniture into the open air it struck him that he had never before performed so free an act. Even the risk of discovery, as in snatched sex, contributed to the pleasure. Saliva dried on his tongue.

Dickinson struck a match. It hovered invisible in the acrid sunlight. And went out. In his sweat he had poured petrol on the files of newspaper clippings that underlay the topple of furniture beneath the trees. With a shaking hand he began tossing lit matches at his flyblown years of journalism squashed beneath the possessions of the house. None of it seemed his any longer. And then one match, as he reached out to flick it, caught. And a sudden, silent, hardly visible shaft of rainbow heat hazed in a rush upward, a quick roar of heat that dried his sweat just as it tore into his hair and swathed across his body almost like comfort, until he looked down and saw that his clothes were licking him, and already he could smell the white-hot tar of his skin burning still invisibly against the sun, and he roared across the lawn, salt in his mouth, eyes blind with the flame from his shirt, and plunged over the long sands that he had never seen, the air quivering, past the cottage she had talked about and into the sea she had longed for. His life briefly passed him by. And he burnt to death in the cold waters which his last breath imagined at the edges of his mind.

Was it an accident?

The book did not believe in accidents. People had too deliberate a way of unconsciously chasing their destinies.

Who could argue? The book was itself a growling unconscious, one that had the tenacity of a dog. No one could escape by trying to throw it off.

In any case, by good fortune, a particularly risible element in me had died in the flames: that weakness in refusing to admit emotion, in taking things so far without the daring to push them nearer the brink, in clinging to a career while spitting at it, in giving in to women only to take them vengefully, in avoiding any commitment except to the gross indulgences of the self. I had been very fond of Hugh, a closer friend for many years than I had supposed, but it looked as though the book knew better than I did how much I needed him out of the way. Nothing was an accident.

But where had Lady Fielden gone, poor thing? I wondered. I was now missing her. I had lost a dimension without even identifying it. Her absence worried me. Somewhere I had done her no justice. I hoped she would come back to remark or correct or haunt, long after *The Little Book* was forgotten, if ever.

I returned this afternoon from Ryde on the open-topped double-decker that plied on bright days between us and the pier. It was by far the most exciting approach to Seaview, the wind of excess speed downhill sweeping my eyes half-shut, the scents of dying summer taking my breath away, the hair of the girls blown on end, the views over the treetops rushing past from the heights near Nettlestone to sea-level. In this reckless dash I glimpsed far away on the mainland a shaft of sunlight catching Chichester Cathedral, Portsmouth blacked out by thunder, my knuckles white with elation. I had never felt more alive.

And you saw it.

At this stage, darling, as *The Little Book* moved towards the end, I knew that Owen William Parry had been disappointed by his one-man campaign to alert London to notions of change. Nobody he knew could afford the book, and when he distributed free copies, stolen from the warehouse, nobody wanted it; in that proud area gifts were viewed as worthless. A few irresponsibles had taken his advice to walk out of work and risk all. But in Parry's district nobody could move more than a little way without risking too much. The very existence of society rendered its reform impossible. Nor did anyone actually want to leave home. They liked dying as close as possible to their place of birth.

Owen Parry despaired. Should he set an example? There seemed no choice. Sleepily he looked at the book again. And the book was simply telling him to go home. He felt the same blind compulsion as anyone else. They had all learnt from the book what it probably meant without reading it. By preaching it he had caused a lot of trouble for nothing. It was time to get out.

Until that moment Owen Parry had never

realized how much he wanted to be alone for a long time in a place he understood in his bones. He had never visited Wales since a boy. The place had adhered to his mind like a picture postcard of someone else's happiness. It was a place where streams trickled through rocks from mountains that thunderously fingered the clouds over lanes that wound steeply down between hawthorn hedge or oak forest. A succession of green views opened up. Race memory: a place that ached of tea-times, tingling with a childhood never had, gathering moss, counting sheep in gulleys that sloped in serenity down to rivers expanding into golden estuaries, beyond which the seas of an outside world hammered the shore, a murmur of stones that sermonized and valleys that opened their mouths wide to sing hymns and slate chapels that stood as neat as boxes of truth by the wayside. The land of his fathers had kept his mind in place for years. Trapped him.

One Friday afternoon at the warehouse Parry packed his last parcel. He did not collect his cards. In a gesture he thought futile but necessary he left the office without a word. At that point he passed out of sight of *The Little Book*, needing it no more, and at the same time out of my mind, no longer needing to accommodate him. If all he wanted was to find his father, someone he could trust and work for and revere, good luck to him. He had escaped what he mistook for the challenges by returning to what he thought were his roots. It was a happy death, and I suspected he had never felt more alive. A vast peace descended on Wales, origins, homes, fathers, and all they no longer stood for.

But I was finding it harder to follow Lady Fielden wherever she had vanished after the storm brought down her house. She flicked in and out of my thoughts with the force of a caricature. Wandering across meadows in a cranky search for herbs, intoning a ritual on the crazy heights of the downland, holding hands in the psychic gloom, awaiting voices. I thought of her with regret imprisoned in the occult.

But she also cropped up in dreams, just before I woke, inhabiting old parts of my life – criminal Marseilles, environs of Rome, a London backwater – where I would never have imagined her presence. She slipped into my mind out of alleyways as I walked the Seaview streets, sorting out my own final way of measuring up to the book's demands. Her assurance filled me as my lonely eye faltered over vistas of sea, villa, sky. It was as if she were busy elsewhere but keeping me now and then in mind. Like an intuition. But I could not dislodge her from my still centre. As a person she seemed to have died out of time. But here she was inside me at last.

I sharply knew that one of the many persons I might have been – yes, this woman, brainless, guided by feelings but forced often to deny them, traditional in upbringing but girlishly eager to explore – had not been destroyed by *The Little Book*, but had been disclosed to me, privately, as a result of my reading it. I may have resisted her for years, but here she was, in all innocence, stirring emotion, making me feel, the one side of my character which in fear I had suppressed; thus improving my chances of ecstasy, of advancing a step or two, of leaping into discovery, of falling enough in love with myself to enlarge my capacity to love others, of inducing other people in a similar spirit to read *The Little Book*.

Lady Fielden's vigour was with me. I asked for no more than this last-minute resurrection of a self I might never have gained.

Her better half, alas, had come to grief. The story went that Sir Davis had been consumed by a flood of belated passion. That was one way of putting it. In fact, in the naked gunroom, his heart had given out during the storm. Perhaps, some thought, his heart had never been there in the first place; and at that moment, poignantly, with a rush of guilt, I felt the burden of all the times I had stripped her down, whoever she was, placed her over my knee, spread her wide, splayed her loosely on my body, stood her against furniture and/or just done her: and in some ungainly moral sense, not quite liking it, I was glad that this old codger had died in the act before being drowned, while free of him I looked forward in all innocence to falling in love, for the first time again, with you. It was a pity, though, about that maidservant in the nice black stockings. She too could have grown into a heroine or an ideal, if *The Little Book* had not insisted on her being a martyr to the unbelievable weather that night on the Island.

I had wanted the book to have a large end. It didn't. I also wanted to celebrate the climax of the hour of reading it by proposing to the family a last outing: across the furthest sweep of the Island landscape, seen decades ago with an ache of longing from the windows of Priestley's study at Brook. There it stood, a remaining challenge to energy, an Everest to scale – the uprush of white cliffs capped by springy sward above Tennyson's house leading, with the seas crashing far underfoot, to the promontory above the Needles, from which Marconi released his first wireless signal out to a vessel somewhere off Bournemouth. I had always wanted to walk that height.

But we had left too little time for the venture. Suddenly we were leaving today. Puffing a bit, pulling muscles on the climbs, I would on that walk have rounded off my twentieth century with superb views all ways, south to France, north to home, east to the place of my recovery, west to childhood. Instead, on a warm morning in Seaview when others slept and autumn faintly tinged the air, I strolled up to the allotments and stole a last overripe loganberry from someone's patch. I could have nicked a marrow for all the interest anyone took in my amble.

On the way back, popping as agreed into Watson's for breakfast supplies, I saw disappearing down the High Street the tall storkish figure in glasses – a lawyer, I gathered from local rumour – whose academic life had ended in the drama of a stabbing on an Oxford lawn. At least no perverse side of me had ever wanted to go in for the law. But on the beach as I passed the Yacht Club I waved to a retired bishop, an acquaintance whom I had briefly singled out as an aspect of myself, if necessary. He certainly answered to an underside of my desires never exploited and I rather regretted that *The Little Book* (which had its faults) had never suggested leaving me a blank page or two to print that undeveloped negative within: the Rt Revd David Hughes DD, first primate of all Wight – for once appearing under my own name. And down Bluett Avenue, carrying the shopping with a swagger, I glimpsed slipping into her car a woman who once came to dinner in those first days when I was so exhausted as to be blind to society. I waved again. The distance was against her recognizing me. I wondered, and would never know, whether she, successful in advertising as Davina Darley was as a publisher, had contributed a jot to my creation of the latter's looks.

You were packing. Everyone was packing. The house was at the zenith of a turmoil that would shortly end crammed into suitcases. It did not seem like an end. To leave was closing down one shop with a view to reopening our bigger one: going home to a house shut up for weeks, to heaps of envelopes, calls on the machine, dust and heat, next term. Nobody was quite here at Seaview still; we had already left, only our bodies lagged behind. The sea, the great curative sea, the peace that had lasted almost all month, the sun, were ignored. We were all too busy catching a car ferry that left hours later.

I drifted out into the empty length of Bluett Avenue, which had hidden a murderer, let drunks roll up and down it, lifted my brains out of hospital, and into my mind came the field day which the *Isle of Wight County Press* was to enjoy at the book's expense once I had made my escape. Already their men were fanning out to expose some nutter who claimed to have penned the perfect book. Lots of locals, solicitors, churchmen and the like, were muttering that this crazy might be right, and anyway public relations were taking it up as a natural, and the whole story was about to break when there was little else in the news. The reporter from Ryde was worrying various lies between his teeth. One, how this maverick's book was based on island notables whose privacy must be respected. Two, how insistent the author was on withholding every detail until publication day. Three, how keenly he protected his anonymity.

Ear to the ground, our correspondent in Ryde had also picked up a rumour that at the last moment this author had lost his nerve, or knew he would never honour his intentions, or had to admit his task finally impossible. He was reported as pissing off, full of himself, on the next ferry from Fishbourne to the privacy of the mainland.

We caught the boat in good time without panic. The mood was light, the weather fine. We were going home. We were coming back to sense, to responsibility, to the need for achievement, to the normal. The children whizzed off on differing chases all over the ship, to bar or loo or deck or game. Being at sea, even for forty minutes, was limbo, we were each left alone for a while: a growing sense of the approaching, a fading sense of the left behind. I longed for the crossing to be longer. We rolled off into urban Portsmouth, diesel in the throat.

We drove back to London the same way as the outward trip. Rounding the outskirts of Fareham my puzzle was again with health. Why was I better? The nature of well-being was indefinable. It consisted of having no symptoms. The nature of recovery was to be so gradual as to escape notice. Days after I was appreciably better I had realized with shock that I felt indeed better. Along the way, as we drove through Droxford, were minor irritations which the mind blew up into serious threats. A pain in one testicle at Corhampton meant that the cancer had dropped a few inches. A faint ache in the bladder hinted at metastasis in Warnford.

The surgeon at St Thomas's had told me to expect the worst fast. On the Island other small signs had either interrupted the process of springing back to health or proved it was happening. Staring in the mirror and seeing myself not look myself. Mistaking a day's suntan for fever. Falling down from overstrain or drink, not knowing which. Stopping breathless, growing paranoid. Gazing in rapture at a fuchsia hedge, a boxy garage over the road, a pile-up of clouds, as if for the last time, then identifying the intense pleasure as a portent of health. Being an oldish person at death's door getting steadily younger, elatedly unaware at what point this return to youth would come to a halt; meanwhile time was reversing.

Overall, without my help, the picture was of a mind and spirit finding their own way of bringing back a body that had let both down. Hustle anyone into serious illness, and a capacity to cure billowed out: the imagination working on the condition as rigorously as a doctor. And then on through West Meon towards my birthplace.

On the Isle of Wight I had read *The Little Book* without thinking in one incalculable hour. It told me that I had spent sixty years of doubt and muddle preparing for sixty minutes of easy effort. I had been ill. I had wanted something to help me out of a world in which only I existed. To help me to help anyone who felt as I did. To help me to sail into my future as if I had never been dragged back by my past. To help me to live that past all over again as if indeed it were a future. To help me spit out a bad day and savour a good one. And that single hour of words working did it all.

How had it come about that in the midst of death I was in life? The fact is that *The Little Book*, though short, is continuous. I am making it all the time; I am making it up daily. Each day rewrites with slight variations the entire hour of *The Little Book*. So I am the permanent beneficiary of the satisfaction of carrying out what the anonymous author first asked of me: not just to read the book in an hour, but to impose my own problems on his pages, treating them as glassy blanks in which my own story might be mirrored.

The book is with me on my breakfast table now and goes about with me in a pocket. I take it out to restaurants, give it rides on the tops of buses, escort it to parties where I introduce it to acquaintances, and bring it back at night to lie by the bed. Looking back, I have really no idea of what it still contains. We have conducted an exchange: the book's interior is slowly being transferred to me while I am giving it everything that is in me to give: generosity of response, a pride in myself, an act of love, an expanding awareness of the trajectory and span of life – all of which, in fact, the book told me I possessed in the first place, but had hidden behind the ghosts of other people in me. Skulkers, slackers, fakes, fools, pedants, pricks, whatnots, we all had them in us.

Passing through East Tisted I had to consider how to take *The Little Book* beyond itself, as any ultimate little book would have to do if it were to make its point, get its way. On my last page there would be a genuine feeling in readers that they had

read *The Little Book* with pleasure or made it up
– and not been cheated by literary devices. The
mystery must persist. But logic and propriety
must have been served as well. I should be able to
do this by implying the extent and pleasure of my
own recovery: a recovery that is not just related to
a possibly fatal illness, but to the horror you and I
also generally feel in the face of life. Given this unease, I very much want you to come happy out of
these pages. I require us in the end to feel good.

Then let the book drop.

And sigh with relief.

A moment, please, as we negotiate Alton. Only
you will know whether *The Little Book* appears to
mean anything below the strut of the words;
whether it is of no known value, a flight of fancy,
part of a death-wish, an ample cry of freedom, a
natural spin-off of getting better from an illness, a
love letter to you or just to myself, the last gasp of
a western mind at the end of its tether, an
eleventh-hour effort to leave something of a self
behind, a period piece; whether, as a tool of the
mind to combat the fool of matter, the future will
find it useful.

Summer ebbing around me, I arrived back in
Kennington on the last page to find amidst the
mail a card saying that the Post Office had tried
to deliver a packet in my absence. There was no

indication of its content. I hurried to Crampton Street and found on enquiry that whatever it was had been returned to sender after the statutory three weeks, without a postal record of its provenance being kept. A flush of invalid rage consumed me in sweat at the counter.

What was it, where was it, who was it?

A chunk of my mind could not help believing that the jiffybag contained an advance copy of *The Little Book*, publication having been put back to next month to fan the controversy igniting the issue, or to suppress it at the behest of some upstart mafia, or to print more copies to fulfil the expected demand, or to appease the lads (and lasses) who threatened to sue for being projections of myself.

But the book, no matter who had sent it, was lost in the system somewhere. It would never now come back to me. If it could, if it did, I might readdress it unopened to our children, marked to await their coming of age.

Anyway here they are, dearest, these pages I promised you.